MARTIAL LAW

TIMES OF TURMOIL

BOOK TWO

MARTIAL LAW

BY CHAD DAYBELL

spring creek
BOOK COMPANY
Provo, Utah

ISBN 13: 978-1-932898-99-6
e. 1

Published by:
Spring Creek Book Company
P.O. Box 50355
Provo, Utah 84605-0355

www.springcreekbooks.com

Cover design © Spring Creek Book Company
Cover image © Jakub Kalaska

Printed in the United States of America
Printed on acid-free paper

AUTHOR'S NOTE

As I finished writing the final chapters of this volume, the stories dominating the news were the aftermath of the Boston Marathon bombings, trouble in Syria, Oklahoma tornadoes, and numerous government scandals. I started to worry that this supposedly futuristic series was already slipping into the present day, or even into the past. It does indeed feel like we are heading into difficult times.

I was reminded of the following quote from Brigham Young:

"Do you think there is calamity abroad now among the people? Not much. All we have yet heard and experienced is scarcely a preface to the sermon that is going to be preached. When the testimony of the Elders ceases to be given, and the Lord says to them, "Come home; I will now preach my own sermons to the nations of the earth," all you now know can scarcely be called a preface to the sermon that will be preached with fire and sword, tempests, earthquakes, hail, rain, thunders and lightnings, and fearful destruction.

"What matters the destruction of a few railway cars? You will hear of magnificent cities, now idolized by the people, sinking in the earth, entombing the inhabitants. The sea will heave itself beyond its bounds, engulfing mighty cities. Famine will spread over the nations, and nation will rise up against nation, kingdom against kingdom, and states against states, in our own country and in foreign lands."

(*Journal of Discourses, Vol. 8:123, given on July 15, 1860.*)

That certainly sounds cheerful, doesn't it? But those are the events that must take place before the Saints can move forward and build New Jerusalem in preparation for the Savior's return.

As you know, the first volume in this series, *Evading Babylon*, ended with a cliffhanger. One reviewer called it "a brutal trick." I apologize for that, but I felt I needed to stop the book at that point. I didn't quite understand why until I read the book *Visions of Glory*, which was published a few months later. In that book, a man who goes by the pseudonym Spencer shares what he saw during several near-death experiences.

The part of the book that jumped out at me was Spencer's account of a future earthquake striking the Wasatch Front. I've actually included that earthquake in my previous *Standing in Holy Places* series, but Spencer gave additional information and insights about the earthquake, and I've been able to incorporate many of those descriptions into this book.

Another book that played a key role in the shaping of this novel was Suzanne Freeman's new book *The Spirit of Liberty*. I have included a chapter of that book in the back of this volume. She had the privilege of meeting the Founding Fathers in the Spirit World, and their warnings and counsel for modern Americans should be a must-read for everyone.

I'm grateful for my lovely wife Tammy and our children for their continual support and encouragement, as well as everyone who sends me emails asking when the next volume will be completed. It helps spur me on, and I welcome the feedback!

Chad Daybell
July 2013

THE TURMOIL DEEPENS

As this volume opens, Nathan Foster and Marie Shaw have miraculously reunited in Chicago. They are overjoyed to be back together, but they know their lives will be in danger if they attempt to leave the city.

Meanwhile, Nathan's father Garrett and his stepmother Vanessa have seemingly disappeared somewhere in southern California after traveling there to help Vanessa's relatives following an earthquake.

Marie's parents, Aaron and Carol, are living in Orem, Utah, and are watching over Nathan's half-sister Denise. Aaron continues to work at the National Security Agency's Utah Data Center.

It is now mid-June, and the nation is economically shattered following the bioterror attack orchestrated by China. The Black Flu epidemic has temporarily waned, but millions of Americans have died, and the affects of the illness have impacted every citizen.

The government agency FEMA has responded to the mounting housing problems in the southern United States caused by Hurricane Barton a few weeks earlier, but thousands of citizens are still homeless. The temperatures are rising there, and so are tempers. Infections and common diseases are spreading there due to a lack of medicines.

Despite the nation's overwhelming troubles—including festering political scandals and cover-ups—most media outlets continue to deflect criticism away from the U.S. president and his administration. Instead, smiling news anchors rave about the First Lady's latest hairstyle.

Meanwhile, the officers from the Chip Compliance Authority

1

are becoming increasingly brazen in cracking down harshly on people who didn't have the chip, labeling anyone without one as a fugitive from justice.

China and Russia are biding their time, letting the American economy collapse on itself. The Affordable Care Act that began to be fully implemented in 2014 continues to stymie private businesses and even municipalities, leading to greater underemployment and increased medical costs for most Americans. Meanwhile, the national debt continued to grow exponentially as the federal government continued to borrow money in order to cover their obligations.

All of these events have combined to create an atmosphere of uneasiness and stress within the general population. Pockets of civil unrest are again popping up in the nation's larger cities, including Chicago, where Nathan Foster and Marie Shaw currently find themselves.

Now on with their story.

CHAPTER 1

Nathan Foster sat quietly inside Chicago's Smith Museum of Stained Glass Windows, watching Marie Shaw sleep as sunlight began to lighten the room. It had only been a few hours since he had made his dangerous journey across the darkened city and found her hiding there.

Nathan had barricaded the door behind them and then they had talked for nearly an hour. Marie told him about the chaos that erupted in Chicago after the U.S. president's announcement about travel restrictions due to the Black Flu, and Nathan shared how he had miraculously made his way from Utah to find her.

Marie had eventually put her head on his shoulder and drifted off into an exhausted slumber. Nathan had only slept for a couple of hours, though. Every creak or shout outside the building had put him on edge. His confrontation with some street thugs just before finding Marie had bothered him. He had shot one of them in the leg, and even though he doubted the gang could ever identify him, he dreaded going back out on the streets.

Now that the sun had risen, Nathan could clearly see Marie's face for the first time in months. She was still beautiful, but she looked gaunt and pale, compared to the radiant, healthy girl he had last seen in Utah. Her current appearance was likely caused by her lack of food and sunlight for the past week, but she had hinted that her internship had been stressful and demanding, and he suspected that had taken a toll on her as well.

He hated to wake her, but they had agreed to leave the museum as soon as it was daylight. It would likely be the safest time to travel through the city, because all of the troublemakers would hopefully still be asleep after another night of mayhem.

Nathan put his hand on Marie's shoulder and shook her gently. "Marie, it's time for us to get going."

She opened her eyes, sat up, then looked around in a panic before focusing on Nathan's face. She reached out and touched his cheek.

"Oh, you're really here," she said. "It wasn't a dream."

Nathan smiled. "Yep, and we're going to get home somehow."

"You look so worn out," she said. "Did you get any sleep?"

"I dozed off for a couple of hours, but I'm anxious to get out of here."

"Me too, "Marie said. "I'm starving."

"The problem is I don't know Chicago very well," Nathan said. "As you slept I've been praying for a solution, but nothing has come to mind. Any ideas?"

Marie crinkled her brow. "I dreamed we should return to my apartment in the Bloomingdale's Building. Do you think that's our answer?"

Nathan was surprised at her response. "Last night you told me that you'd been warned to leave there immediately because your life was in danger."

"I did get that prompting, but I think that time has passed," she said. "As terrible as it sounds, I'm sure my co-workers have killed each other by now. Besides, I had a couple of boxes of pork and beans stashed under my bed that I doubt anyone found, even if they ransacked the place."

"Pork and beans?"

She smiled sheepishly. "I know it's stupid, but it's always been my comfort food. So I bought a few cases when I first got here and ate a can every couple of days."

"I'm hungry enough that it's got my mouth watering already," Nathan said. "That sounds good to me."

They gathered up their meager belongings, and Nathan double-checked the area with his microchip scanner to see if anyone was nearby, but he didn't detect anyone. They unblocked the doorway and Nathan peered outside across Navy Pier. He could see a few people at the far end of the pier looking across Lake Michigan, so they cautiously slipped out of the museum.

"I don't think they saw us," Marie said as she took Nathan's hand and began a quick trot in the direction of the Bloomingdale's Building. They had been right—the city was quiet, but there were a lot of disturbing scenes along the way. As they reached Michigan Avenue and looked at the long row of skyscrapers, they could see that most of the buildings had been damaged, and some were simply burned-out metal husks. Even more upsetting were the dozens of bodies along the sidewalk and in the streets. Some looked like they had either jumped from or been thrown out of the buildings that towered above them.

"This is terrible," Marie said, shielding her eyes and covering her nose and mouth to help avoid breathing the scent of death that surrounded them. Nathan put his arm around her shoulder.

"I just hope your building didn't burn down," he said.

Twenty minutes later they stood outside the Bloomingdale's Building. The magnificent structure now stood dark and was a bit foreboding, but at least it was intact. They crossed through the building's main entrance, and Marie looked baffled.

"What's wrong?" Nathan asked.

She shook her head. "This is crazy. It's hard to believe it was only a week ago I had to fight my way through a frenzied crowd to even get outside. Where do you think everyone went?"

"I'll bet they stripped the stores and restaurants bare within a couple of days, so they've moved on to find food somewhere else. I'll bet the suburbs are a madhouse right now. People are probably getting very hungry and desperate."

Marie shuddered and took his hand. She led him to the far corner of the building where the staircase was located.

"I really wish the elevator was working," Marie said. "But now there's only one way up."

"What floor is your apartment on?" Nathan asked.

"The 26th," she said.

Nathan's eyes widened. "At least it isn't at the top. Do you think you can make it?"

Marie's strength was already ebbing. Her initial surge of adrenaline from being out on the city streets had worn off, and her pace had slowed considerably.

"I can do it," she said. "I can taste those pork and beans already."

She made a valiant effort, but by the 10th floor she could hardly lift her foot to the next stair. Nathan finally just scooped her into his arms and carried her upward.

After taking several breaks to rest, they finally staggered out of the stairwell onto the 26th floor. Marie slipped from Nathan's arms and motioned toward her apartment. The door was open, and they could see into the front room. The couch had been flipped over and the TV was gone.

As they walked carefully into the apartment they could see the kitchen was in disarray, but Marie's bedroom looked okay.

"Check under the bed," she told him. Nathan crouched down and saw a couple of cardboard boxes still hidden away.

"I think we're in business," he said as he pulled the boxes into the middle of the bedroom floor.

Marie gave a squeal of delight and pulled a can opener from a kitchen drawer. She opened a can, and basically drank half of it within five seconds.

"Hey, how about sharing?" he asked.

"Open one for yourself," she said before putting the can to her mouth again.

Nathan smiled and grabbed another can. Soon he was feasting as well. Their faces were covered with sauce, but they didn't care.

"Oh, it's so good," Marie said as she sat on the edge of the bed and rubbed her stomach.

Nathan nodded as he finished off his can. "I'm just grateful your secret craving wasn't prunes."

She glanced at him and her eyes widened. "Wow, you're quite a sight with those beans in your beard."

Nathan rubbed his face and felt his whiskers. He hadn't shaved since leaving Utah, but it hadn't really crossed his mind that he was growing a beard. He stood up and walked to the bathroom, where he stared into the mirror.

"That's a scary sight," he said as Marie joined him. He brushed the beans away and instinctively turned on the bathroom faucet, but no water came out.

"It's easy to forget how quickly things have changed," he said. "It's like the whole world has turned upside down."

He went to the toilet and took the lid off the tank. "We're in luck," he said. "There's a couple of gallons of water in there. We'll scoop it into another container. Just don't flush it or we'll lose it."

Marie looked surprised. "You're gonna drink that?"

"If we run out of bottled water," he said. "It should still be fairly sanitary. I'll have to be pretty desperate to drink what's in the bowl itself, though."

Marie's eyes suddenly welled up with tears. "I'm so sorry, Nathan. This is all my fault."

"What do you mean?"

"You know what I'm talking about. We're trapped here because of my own foolishness. I honestly thought it was impossible for your 'doomsday scenario' to take place this summer. When you and Dad would talk about it, I just laughed inside. My whole focus was on graduating in December and getting a great job, but that seems so meaningless now."

Nathan looked away. He had vowed not to mention why they were trapped in Chicago. He was ready to just move forward. "It's okay, Marie. Don't beat yourself up about it."

She wiped her eyes then looked at him pleadingly. "I do want you to know this experience has changed me."

"What has? The internship?"

"Yes, but also the past few days hiding in the museum, expecting to die. I've done more praying in the past week than I have the past few years. My priorities are straightened out. I hope you can forgive me for how I've acted."

"Certainly," Nathan said. "I see your point of view. You were on the brink of a successful career. I wish it had worked out."

She nodded, unsure how to respond.

"One other thing," he said hesitantly. "I enjoyed hugging and kissing you when we reunited last night, but I need to let you know I've been set apart again as a missionary, and so for now, I need to act like one."

"I completely understand," Marie said. Then she mischievously added, "Just keep that filthy beard. That will keep me away."

CHAPTER 2

Aaron Shaw sat down at his desk in the National Security Agency's Utah Data Center in Bluffdale, Utah, and quickly logged onto his computer. Nathan had departed four days earlier to find Marie in Chicago, and he hadn't heard anything from him.

This wasn't a surprise, because they had agreed not to call each other. Marie seemed determined to stay hidden in the museum on Navy Pier, so the only way Aaron would know if Nathan had reached Marie was if her chip indicated she'd left the building.

Within moments he called up her profile and was surprised to discover she was back in her apartment in the Bloomingdale's Building. Nathan must have found her! Aaron uttered a silent prayer of gratitude.

"They must be getting some supplies that she'd stored away," he told himself, hoping some of his preparedness lessons during Family Home Evening over the years had actually rubbed off on his daughter.

Aaron would've gladly sat and watched that little dot on his screen all morning, but he had other urgent tasks to complete. When Marie first took the Chicago internship, Aaron had been given permission by his boss to check on her occasionally. However, ever since the Black Flu outbreak had spread across the nation, Aaron's department had been swamped with assignments. He was sure his boss would revoke the privilege if he remembered giving it, so Aaron would just have to be cautious about it.

He couldn't resist calling his wife Carol, though. He dialed their home number and Carol answered.

"She's okay," he said quietly, and he heard Carol begin to cry with relief on the other end of the line. He knew Carol was aware he didn't dare say anything else for security reasons, so he simply hung up and moved forward with his next assignment.

This assignment wasn't one he enjoyed. He had the task of evaluating the chip status of people who had been admitted to large hospitals within the Los Angeles earthquake zone. The federal government had convinced the news outlets that the fatalities in southern California from the combination of the earthquake and the Black Flu were quite low, but in reality the totals were staggering.

The NSA computers crunched the numbers and provided the data, but there were still some cases where a human had to analyze the circumstances to determine if the people were actually dead. If they had simply removed their chips, they were considered fugitives and the Chip Compliance Authority was alerted.

Aaron was currently working through the admittance records for Huntington Memorial Hospital in Pasadena, California. He had two windows open on his screen. One showed a list of people who had been admitted to the hospital in the days after the earthquake, while in the other window he would enter each person's chip ID number and see their current status.

If a person was alive, the word "Awake" would show on the screen, while a deceased person's chip reading showed "Asleep."

This politically-correct labeling had irritated Aaron at first, but he realized that it was almost as if the government couldn't bring themselves to say the word "dead" even though a sizable portion of the nation's population was now in that category.

He worked his way down the list for about an hour, and nearly all of the patients' chips registered "Asleep" with no indication of foul play. According to the GPS devices embedded in their chips, nearly all of the deceased people were in the same area—a parking lot outside the hospital. He shook his head, trying not to picture the grotesque scene there. There were reports coming in from many California cities of bodies being literally stacked outside hospitals and left to rot. The number of Americans who had died in just the past two weeks was staggering.

Aaron paused for a moment to check again on Marie. She was in her apartment, and he could picture Nathan watching over her. He yearned for a way to contact them. It was gut-wrenching to not be able to know what was actually going on. He delved back into his work, and after five minutes he came to a name on the list of hospital patients that made him jump.

Vanessa Foster — Orem, Utah.

"Isn't that Nathan's stepmother?" he whispered. He knew Nathan's parents had gone to California to help her relatives after the earthquake, and their daughter Denise hadn't heard from them in a few days. In fact, Denise was currently staying with them because she feared her parents were dead.

Aaron's fingers trembled as he entered Vanessa's chip ID number, and his heart sank as the dreaded word appeared: "Asleep."

Aaron clicked on her photo that was taken when she received the chip, and it was indeed her. He knew he'd have to tell Denise the truth when he returned home that evening. He hated to do it, but it would help ease her suffering. She had been tormented by not knowing for sure what had happened to her mother.

On Vanessa's screen was a link to her husband Garrett, Nathan and Denise's father. "I guess I'll confirm his status while I'm at it so I can let them know," Aaron thought.

He entered Garrett's ID number and the word "Awake" appeared. Aaron shook his head and slowly typed in the number again. The computer immediately responded, "Awake."

"That can't be right," Aaron said.

He opened a third window and checked on all of Garrett's recent chip interactions. He'd been admitted to the same Pasadena hospital that Vanessa had, but there weren't any other records for him beyond that.

Aaron was stumped. "If he's alive, where is he?"

He clicked on a "chip locator" button that linked directly to Google Earth. The center of the screen zoomed down toward

California, positioned itself over Pasadena, and then focused on a motionless dot in a parking lot outside Huntington Memorial Hospital.

"That's crazy," Aaron said. "How is he not dead?"

CHAPTER 3

❧

Garrett Foster felt a deep pounding in his head, and his entire body ached. It felt like he was lying on pavement. He could hear the buzzing of flies around him, and as he took a deep breath he was assaulted by a mixture of foul odors.

He opened his eyes and saw a blue sky above him, and then he turned his head just enough to see a nearby sign that read "Huntington Memorial Hospital."

He vaguely remembered Vanessa frantically driving him to an emergency room in Pasadena. "Vanessa!" he cried out hoarsely. "Where are you?"

With great difficulty he raised up on one elbow and looked around him. Terror filled his chest as he saw he was in the midst of hundreds of dead bodies spread across a parking lot. Some bodies were covered with sheets, but most of them appeared as if they had been unceremoniously dragged there and abandoned.

Garrett looked at his hands, which were covered with dark blotches. Had he somehow survived the Black Flu? He swatted at the flies landing on his face and staggered to his feet. Thankfully, the people who had dumped the bodies had left a small path across the parking lot.

He walked slowly along, looking at the corpses around him in hopes of seeing Vanessa, but most of the bodies were decomposing and were hard to even look at. Finally he picked up his pace toward the shade of a tree in a grassy strip along the parking lot. He barely made it before a wave of nausea engulfed him. He collapsed on the grass, feeling so miserable that he could only close his eyes and moan. For a brief moment he wished to be dead like everyone else around him, but he sensed there was a purpose that he was still alive. For the first time in years he cried out in sincere prayer.

"Dear Father, I suppose I deserve this torment. Let me die if it is thy will. Otherwise, direct me where to go."

As he said those words, he looked under a nearby bush and saw a Gatorade bottle. He crawled over to it and was astounded to find it was unopened. He cracked the lid and sipped it slowly. It was warm and salty, but it was like manna from heaven to him.

Within a few minutes he felt stronger, and he stood up to get his bearings. He didn't know Pasadena very well. Vanessa had actually done all of the driving once they had reached California, since she knew the area better than he did. He doubted he could find her siblings' houses again even if he remembered the addresses.

He leaned against the tree in despair. His memory of what had happened since they left Utah was so foggy he hardly trusted it. All he knew was he was alive, and Vanessa was probably dead. He could hardly comprehend life without her.

Clang. Clang. Clang.

Garrett turned and saw a disheveled man riding a bicycle down the middle of the street toward him. Four metal watering cans were hanging from the bike's handlebars, banging into each other and making the racket. When he was within twenty yards, Garrett called out, "Hey! Over here!"

The man slammed on his brakes so fast he nearly went over the handlebars. He climbed off the bike and pulled a knife from his pocket. "What do you want?" he shouted.

Garrett held his hands out as a sign of peace. "I don't want any trouble. I've been sick and I don't know what's going on. Can you help me?"

The man shook his head. "Stay away. I'm just going to get water for my family."

"That's fine, but where is everyone?"

The man shrugged. "They're gone. A lot of people died, and those who could got out of here once the flu started to spread. I heard there are some people living by the ocean, though."

"It just seems hard to believe," Garrett said. "There were millions of people here."

The man frowned. "Not anymore. Don't go downtown. I heard it turned into a bloodbath as things got worse. People were fighting over everything. It's terrible."

"Worse than this?" Garrett said, pointing to the parking lot.

"Yes."

Garrett shook his head at how society had seemingly collapsed so quickly. He pointed at the cans dangling from the handlebars. "Where are you going to get the water?"

The man's face hardened. "None of your business." He started pedaling away, and Garrett helplessly watched him disappear around the corner.

Garrett walked to the front of the hospital, hoping to find a doctor or nurse, but all he found was more dead bodies. He imagined the hospital staff had become so overwhelmed they had finally just fled to preserve their own sanity and find their own families.

He wasn't sure how long he'd gone without food, but he sensed his body starting to shut down. He was going to die if he didn't find something to eat soon. Garrett remembered the man had said something about the ocean. All he could think of was endless salt water, but maybe people were catching fish there. He started walking west, knowing he'd find the seashore eventually.

"What have I got to lose?" he muttered. "I'll just follow the sun."

CHAPTER 4

After eating their pork and beans, Nathan and Marie weren't sure whether to leave immediately or stay in the apartment. Nathan was silently praying for some inspiration, but he knew the first priority was to give Marie more time to regain her strength. She was near the breaking point, both physically and mentally.

He pointed to the bedroom. "We're safe now. I really think you just need to take a long nap."

Marie gave a sigh of relief. "Thank you. I'm not sure I actually slept more than a couple hours at a time when I was in the museum. There were too many people shouting, even in the middle of the night."

She went to the bedroom and collapsed on the bed, while Nathan pulled up a chair next to the window in the living room. He had a fairly clear view of Michigan Avenue, and he saw a surprising number of people walking along, but most seemed to be wandering aimlessly.

Nathan was more concerned about a growing column of black smoke about a mile away that was blowing in their direction. It appeared as if an entire city block was burning. He expected to hear sirens, but there was only an eerie silence.

After about a half hour of looking out the window, Nathan couldn't keep his eyes open. He tipped the couch upright again and dozed on it for a while, but a noise jolted him back awake. He sat up and realized someone was jostling the door knob to the apartment. Out of habit, he had locked the door and latched the chain when they first entered the apartment, and now he was glad he had. He slid off the couch and kneeled behind it, pulling the pistol from his pocket.

The door popped open, but the chain latch only allowed it to open six inches. To Nathan's astonishment, a man called out, "Hello, Marie? I'm here to help you."

Nathan glanced toward Marie in the bedroom, but she didn't stir at all. He almost rushed to her side, but then he felt compelled to stay put and keep quiet.

Crack!

Nathan instinctively ducked his head as the man kicked in the door, ripping the chain from the wall. Nathan could hear footsteps as the man made a direct line toward the bedroom.

Nathan jumped up and pointed the gun at the man's chest. "Stop right there!"

The man froze and put his hands in the air. "Hey, hold on! Don't shoot. I'm with the Chip Compliance Authority. I am just checking on Marie Shaw's status."

Nathan was glad he had a gun, because the guy was about 6'4" and solid muscle. He spotted something in the intruder's right hand. At first he thought it was a gun, but then he recognized it as a microchip detector.

The commotion had awakened Marie, who called out, "Nathan? Are you all right? What's going on?"

"Come out and join me, Marie," Nathan said. "We've got an unwelcome visitor."

Marie peered out of the bedroom and saw the CCA officer standing there. She hurried to Nathan's side, and he handed her the pistol.

"Shoot him in the chest several times if he doesn't do as I say," Nathan said.

"Hey, I'm not looking for trouble," the man said nervously. "I'm just doing my job. I could get you locked away for assaulting an officer."

"That's true, but I'll take the risk," Nathan said, "Please drop your chip detector and then turn your pockets inside out."

The man frowned, but as Marie took a step toward him with the pistol, he dropped the device and then emptied his pockets. Two switchblades fell out, along with a set of keys.

As Marie kept the gun trained on the man, Nathan picked up the items off the floor. He examined the set of keys and realized they were master keys to most styles of locks.

"That's how you got in here so easily," Nathan said. He went back to Marie and took the pistol from her as the man watched them warily. Nathan sensed the officer was poised to run out of the apartment.

"Why don't you sit on the floor," Nathan told him. "I promise we'll let you go if you'll just answer some questions."

The man sneered. "Promises are hollow. Why should I tell you anything?"

Nathan stared angrily into the man's eyes. "Because I promise you won't leave here alive if you don't cooperate."

The man's eyes widened, then he slowly sat down in the middle of the front room. Marie glanced over at Nathan with admiration. She hadn't seen this side of him before.

"What's your name?" Nathan asked.

"Shawn."

"What's your assignment with the CCA?" Nathan asked.

"I'm helping with the big roundup—bringing in the strays, so to speak. Haven't you heard about it?"

Nathan shook his head. "Tell us what's going on."

Shawn shrugged. "With all of the shortages of food and medicine, the government wants to get everyone together so they can make good decisions about how to divide things up. They don't want anyone hiding and hoarding things that could benefit everyone else. You know—martial law."

"Has the president actually declared martial law?" Nathan asked.

"Not yet, but all of the laws are in place to make the switch," Shawn said. He nodded toward the boxes of pork and beans. "For example, I'll need to confiscate those boxes from you."

"Good luck with that," Marie said. "Nathan, give me one of those knives."

As Nathan handed one to her, Shawn just chuckled. "You aren't going to get away with this. They'll suspect something strange is going on with me pretty soon. They'll trace my detector and send Brix's guys to find me. You won't stand a chance against them."

"Brix?" Nathan asked. "Who's that?"

Shawn looked at him strangely. "Where have you two been? Living in a cave?"

"I suppose you could say that," Nathan said. "Now answer my question."

"Brix pretty much runs this city," Shawn said. "He started a few years ago as a small-time gang leader, but now he's got more power than the mayor. Everyone is intimidated by him because he kills first and asks questions later. So the federal government decided it would be best to bring him into the CCA fold if they wanted to avoid total chaos here."

"What caused all of the problems?" Nathan asked. "The Black Flu?"

"Not really," Shawn said. "It didn't spread here as bad as it has in California and New York where all those millions of people have died, but everyone was still upset by the president's announcement about travel restrictions."

"We knew about that," Marie said, "but is that really what caused everyone to go nuts?"

"The other trigger last week was when rumors started flying that the government was going to drop the food-stamp program and cut off unemployment benefits."

Marie nodded. "Yes, that would do it."

Shawn shrugged and kept talking casually, seemingly forgetting he had a pistol pointed at his chest. "This city has been on the verge of an explosion for years, and this finally set it off. The National Guard and the cops were overwhelmed during the riots, so Brix's guys became the enforcers. It's the survival of the fittest now."

Nathan was bothered to hear that the government was

cooperating with criminals to keep the peace, but it really wasn't surprising.

"It's my turn for a question," Shawn said. "Where's your chip? When I came up here, the detector only showed hers. When did you remove it? I could throw you in jail for that offense alone."

"I never got one," Nathan said.

Shawn looked stunned. "How have you never got caught?"

Nathan ignored the question and turned to Marie. "Do you have a rope or something we can tie him up with? We need to get out of here without him on our trail."

As Nathan kept the gun pointed at Shawn, Marie went to a closet, pulled out a vacuum cleaner, and cut off the cord. "Will this work?"

Nathan nodded. "That should do."

For the first time, Shawn looked uncomfortable. "Hey, let's talk this out. You guys can take off, and I'll divert Brix's guys when they come."

"I wish I could believe you," Nathan said. "Lay down on your stomach. When Brix's men arrive, they can untie you."

Shawn glared at them, then slowly did as he was told. Nathan tied his hands tightly together behind his back, but as he lifted Shawn's ankle, the larger man swiftly pivoted and kicked Nathan powerfully in the chest, knocking him down. Shawn then squirmed to his feet and ran toward the door. Marie fired off an awkward shot that hit the wall, and then he was gone.

Nathan got up and ran into the hall, where he could hear Shawn's footsteps hurriedly retreating down the staircase. He returned to the apartment, where Marie was still holding the pistol but shaking badly. Nathan gently took the gun from her, then took her in his arms and held her tightly.

"I'm sorry," he said. "I let my guard down with him. We just need to leave immediately."

Marie started to cry. "What's the point? He'll be back with Brix's men soon, and they'll find us the same way he did—my chip. We've only got one choice. Let's cut it out right now."

Nathan hesitated. "If we get separated, it's how I'll find you again. Plus, your dad is keeping tabs on us this way."

Even as Nathan said it, though, he knew it needed to be done. He looked her in the eyes, and she didn't show any fear.

"Do it," she said. "Hurry. We're wasting time."

He rushed to the bathroom and found an unused shaving razor. He broke it apart and brought the blade back to the kitchen, along with a big bandage he found in the medicine cabinet.

Marie was sitting nervously with her right hand resting flat on the table. "See that little scar on the back?" she asked. "That's the spot to cut."

She looked away as Nathan carefully made a quarter-inch slice in the back of her hand. It began to bleed instantly as he pinched both sides of the cut and felt the chip under some tissue just below the surface. He used the razor again to get under it and cut it free, causing Marie to gasp in pain.

"I got it out," Nathan said, placing the tiny chip in his palm. "I know that hurt."

Marie bit her lip and pressed down on the cut with her other hand. "Yeah, I'm going to need that bandage," she said.

Nathan helped her get the bandage in place, and the bleeding stopped quickly. He couldn't resist kissing her on the forehead. "Good job," he told her. "That was very brave."

Marie took the chip from him, put it on the floor and crushed it to bits under her shoe. When she was finished it looked like a squashed bug.

Shawn's chip detector was still on the table, along with the other switchblade. Nathan pocketed the knife and set of keys, then picked up the tracking device. It was similar to the one he had been using, but Shawn had mentioned that it could be tracked, unlike the first-edition version Nathan had that was undetectable.

"We'll leave it here on the table for Brix's men to find," he said. "That will hopefully keep them off our trail."

Marie went to her bedroom and returned with a small suitcase that had wheels and an extendable handle. "Should we load this up with the cans of pork and beans?" she asked. "I really don't want to leave them behind."

"Great idea," Nathan said. They were able to fit the remaining cans into the suitcase, as well as some bottled water Marie had also stashed under the bed.

Nathan checked the stairway, listening for any sounds, but it was quiet. The suitcase was heavy, but his adrenaline was pumping, and he easily picked it up.

"Let's go," he said to Marie. "Stay right behind me."

They hurried down the stairs, and it seemed like an eternity as the floor numbers slowly ticked backward. When they reached the 10th floor, Nathan needed to put the suitcase down.

"I've been thinking that we shouldn't just burst out the front door," Marie said. "They might be waiting for us."

"That's true," Nathan said. "What do you suggest?"

"Let's wait on the second floor. There's a clothing store near the stairway we could hide in for a little while. That way we'll hear if they're going up the stairs for us."

Nathan picked up the suitcase again, and within five minutes they were stepping through the broken glass of the store's front display window. The shelves were nearly bare.

"I guess even in tough times, you need to loot some high-priced skirts," Marie said.

Nathan spotted an oversized wheelchair that had been abandoned in the store, and an idea formed in his head.

"I think I've found our way out of Chicago," he said. "We'll put the suitcase on the wheelchair's footpads, and then I'll push you like you're on the verge of dying. I'm sure we can find some clothes in here to help disguise us."

While Nathan found some frumpy hats and a blanket they could use, Marie went behind a sales counter, where she found a large piece of cardboard and a Sharpie. She wrote in big letters: *Black Flu victim! Please help me!*

Nathan smiled. "That should keep people away."

They heard a commotion in the stairwell, and Nathan joined

Marie to hide behind the counter. He carefully peeked around it and saw four men zoom past as they headed up the stairs.

"What floor are we going to?" a man called out.

"The 26th," a familiar voice responded.

Marie shook her head and whispered, "Shawn."

Nathan nodded. "Let's give them 30 seconds, then we better get out of here."

They crept out of their hiding spot behind the counter and listened as the men climbed higher up the stairwell. Finally they nodded at each other and piled all of their items in the wheelchair's seat. Then they carefully took it over to the stairwell and quietly worked together to get it down the stairs one step at a time.

When they reached the main floor, Marie quickly got situated in the wheelchair with her feet on the suitcase. They put the hats on their heads, then Nathan draped the blanket around her shoulders and propped the sign on her lap.

"I think we're ready," Nathan said. "I hope they didn't leave a lookout behind."

They cautiously rolled out onto the sidewalk, then moved to the middle of the street where they were the least likely to encounter anyone. Once in a while someone would shout at them from a window, and each time Nathan would call out, "Please help us! My friend has the Black Flu. Do you have any food you could share?"

There wouldn't be a response back. They also occasionally passed people who were loitering in front of a building and seemingly looking for trouble, but Marie would just shift the "Black Flu" sign so they could read it, and they would move away without even making eye-contact.

Nathan soon got off Michigan Avenue and took several side streets deeper into the city to get further away from Lake Michigan, where a lot of people were now congregating.

"As the days go by, that's probably going to be their only water source," Nathan whispered.

Nathan had considered two possible places they could go, but as he looked at the billowing black smoke to the north, he ruled out the Chicago Temple. Judging by the smoke in the air, it really looked like the northern section of the city was going up in flames. So Nathan pushed Marie south. Their destination was nearly 300 miles away, but it seemed like the only place they'd find safety.

"Where are we going?" Marie finally asked.

"Nauvoo."

Chapter 5

Garrett Foster had made slow but steady progress toward the Pacific Ocean from Pasadena over the past few hours. He had followed the road signs to Interstate 10, which seemed to be leading him to the city of Santa Monica. He had been there once, and while he didn't expect it to be the fun coastal town he remembered, it couldn't be worse than what he'd seen since waking up in that hospital parking lot.

He was surprised he didn't have an appetite, which was good, since he hadn't found any food along the way. He was constantly thirsty, though. He had held onto his Gatorade bottle, and anytime he saw a culvert passing under the freeway, he checked for water. Most of the time he could find a small puddle.

Sometimes there were tiny larva or other creatures swimming in the water, but he told himself, "Hey, I just survived the Black Flu. What's a bug or two going to do, kill me?"

Garrett had followed the freeway in hopes of having a car pass by so he could hitch a ride, but the only cars he'd seen were abandoned on the road. The pavement had some large cracks in it from the earthquake, so he figured the highway had been shut down.

He knew Hollywood was somewhere nearby, but he sensed there wouldn't be a celebrity sighting anytime soon. In the homes beyond the freeway he had heard sporadic shouts and bangs, so there seemed to be other people out there, but he doubted they were in a welcoming mood. The lights along the freeway never turned on after the sun went down, and darkness quickly surrounded him.

He decided his best bet was to find a car to spend the night in right there on the freeway. He soon spotted a white minivan ahead and decided it might work to sleep in if he could fold down the back seats. He pulled on the van's passenger-door handle, and it opened, but he was greeted by a terrible odor. He peered in and then recoiled. A male corpse was sitting there with his head slumped down, still strapped into his seat belt. There were symptoms of the Black Flu clearly evident on the man's face and arms.

Garrett slammed the door closed. Maybe the man's family had been taking him to a hospital and never made it. Garrett sat down in the road in shock and sadness. For brief moments during his walk he had felt like things were almost normal, but then the reality of the situation always came rushing back.

He shook off the horror of the minivan and noticed a small evergreen tree a few yards off the road. He stumbled over to it and wiggled underneath the branches. It wasn't comfortable, but he was so exhausted he fell asleep almost immediately.

When the sun rose, Garrett awoke feeling surprisingly stronger. As he walked west once again, he was caught off guard when the story of Coriantumr, the last Jaredite, popped into his mind. He couldn't help but smile, because although he hadn't read the Book of Mormon in years, he could certainly relate to the loneliness that Coriantumr must have felt after his civilization had fallen apart. Just a few weeks earlier the Los Angeles area had been filled with millions of people, and now everyone had seemingly disappeared.

By noon Garrett had reached the Santa Monica city limits, and up ahead he saw some sort of barrier across the freeway. As he got closer he could see that several cars had been pushed together to form a blockade. Two men stood in the road. They had spotted him, and one of the men pulled a rifle from one of the cars.

"What can you offer us?" the taller man said.

"I've got $3,000 in my bank account—if you can find an ATM

that works. You can have it all if you'll let me get to the ocean."

The taller man chuckled. "You'd be lucky to get a loaf of bread for that much around here."

Garrett stared at them. "Are things really that bad? I was out of commission with the flu for a while."

"I'm afraid so," the shorter man said. "You're not still contagious, are you?"

"I don't think so. I feel pretty good. I just walked here from Pasadena."

"That's impressive," the taller one said. "What are your skills? Can you fish?"

"Absolutely. I'll fish all day."

The men turned away from Garrett, but he could still hear their conversion.

"What do you think?" one of them asked. "Sergeant Casey said we needed more men down on the pier."

Garrett's ears perked up. "Did you say Sergeant Casey? Layne 'Spacey' Casey?"

Both men spun around. "How did you know that?" the taller one asked.

Garrett smiled. "I spent a year in Iraq with him. I knew he was from southern California, but who would've thought we'd meet up again?"

"Well, it sounds like you're in luck," the taller man said. "This exit will take you to Cloverfield Boulevard. Follow it for a couple of blocks and you'll see a Ralphs grocery store. Tell the woman there that you're a longtime friend of Sergeant Casey. I wouldn't mention his nickname, though."

"Thank you," Garrett said, actually half-bowing to the men. "I'm so grateful."

They merely nodded and motioned Garrett toward the exit ramp. Once he got off the freeway, he saw several people outside, and Garrett had to admit it reminded him of a hippie commune. People were unbathed and not wearing much clothing, but they would wave to him as he passed by. An older lady even walked over to him and handed him a piece of bread.

"This is wonderful," he told her after taking a bite. "I haven't eaten in days."

She looked him up and down. "I can tell. You could pass for a really skinny zombie."

Garrett smiled, realizing he was likely an unshaven mess, plus he still had the splotches of the Black Flu on his arms.

"I don't think I'm contagious," he told her.

She waved her hand. "At this point, everyone around here has been exposed. We're a bunch of survivors here. It looks like you had quite a battle with it."

"Well, I woke up in a hospital parking lot among hundreds of dead bodies, so I think you're right."

Garrett looked at the dozen or so people on the street ahead of him. "How is everyone surviving here?" he asked.

"We just get along," the woman said. "It's as if the rest of the world has forgotten about us. We haven't had electricity here since the earthquake, so the men spend their days fishing, and the women cook up whatever they catch."

"I'm looking for Sergeant Casey. He's an old friend. The guards on the freeway said he's in a Ralphs grocery store. Can you take me there?"

"Follow me," she said, leading him down the street. "So you know the sergeant? Thank goodness he took control here, or we might have ended up like everyone else."

"What did he do to help you?"

"First of all, he was on our city council, so he was already well-known by the citizens. When the mayor died in the earthquake, the sergeant immediately took control, and within hours we had sealed off our city. With his military background, he was a natural leader. The smartest thing he did was lock down the grocery stores. This prevented the troublemakers from looting everything, and that has helped us stay fed. Then when the flu swept through, we suffered like everyone else and lost a lot of people, but at least we were organized and had the geography working in our favor."

"What do you mean?"

She motioned toward the sea. "We had the ocean to our backs, and we gathered everyone onto this side of Interstate 10 so we could use it as a protective wall against any mobs coming from the south. Then to our north is Topanga State Park, so not many people came from that direction. All we had to do was stop everyone as they came toward us on the freeway."

Garrett looked around. "I'm glad I made it through. I've seen nothing but misery until now."

They walked along the sidewalk and soon stood in front of the grocery store. "Here we are," she said. "I didn't catch your name."

"I'm Garrett. And you?"

"Neva. I'm sure we'll see each other again soon."

Garrett approached the door, where another woman stood guard. She had a frown on her face and looked like she could bodyslam him, but Garrett wasn't worried. He had a code word up his sleeve he knew would work like a charm.

"I'm here to see Sergeant Casey," he said confidently. "Please tell him Garrett 'The Ferret' Foster is here."

The woman hardly had time to turn around before they heard a man call out, "Ferret Foster? In the flesh? Unbelievable!"

Within moments, Garrett was in the crushing embrace of his old Army pal. Layne soon stepped back and stared at him.

"Hey man, you look . . . you look awful."

Garrett grinned. "You're right! But hopefully I can help you out here and get some meat back on my bones."

Layne looked over at the unsmiling woman. "He's fine. If you can't trust Ferret Foster, you can't trust anyone."

Layne led him back into the store and said, "Choose anything you want, but I'll bet a hamburger would taste good to you."

Garrett's eyes bulged out. "You've got a hamburger? Have I died and gone to heaven?"

Layne laughed. "Ferret, I've missed you."

As Garrett filled his stomach over the next ten minutes, the pair got reacquainted.

"Maybe you remember I'm from Utah," Garrett said. "Any chance of getting back there?"

"I wouldn't count on it," Layne said. "The last thing I heard was I-15 was shut down through the mountains, and Las Vegas was out of control. I'd just stay here for now. I've got a shortwave radio that I charge up with a solar panel, and I've been able to contact a few people. This is certainly turning into the 'Summer of Discontent' across the country."

⤞

Later that afternoon Layne took Garrett down to the Santa Monica Pier. Large portions of it had crumbled into the sea, but people had nailed together some boards and plywood so they could still make their way out onto it. Garrett saw a dozen guys standing on the pier, casting their fishing lines. Some were reeling in fish even as they watched.

"I'll fish for you all day, every day," Garrett said. "Just let me keep a couple of them to eat."

"Eat all you want," Layne said. "I'm glad you're here."

CHAPTER 6

Aaron Shaw pondered how his career had taken him to this point. His first assignment after leaving Novell and joining the National Security Agency had involved a top-secret program called PRISM, which included collecting information from companies such as Apple, Facebook and Google.

After the public found out about PRISM in 2013, he was switched to another department in preparation for the release of the chip. The government was worried that the turmoil about PRISM would cause a backlash to the chip, but most Americans didn't seem to mind that the government was tracking their every move, so the program continued on.

In some ways, the PRISM scandal worked in the federal government's favor, because the NSA leaders realized there wasn't going to be much of an uproar about the chip. The government had spent billions of dollars over the previous decade to track citizens' various social media and email usage, but the chip had simplified everything. Now anyone using the chip literally couldn't even go to the restroom without the government knowing about it.

Aaron had been part of the smooth marketing campaign that introduced the chip, and he even came up with a few of the more popular slogans, such as, *"Parents, do you know where your kids are? Get the chip, and you always will!"*

Aaron personally detested the whole concept, but he knew he had an important role to fulfill, because he was able to keep the LDS Church leaders informed about what the government was planning and how evil the chip program truly was.

When he finally received the chip, he was worried the government would easily find out he was working as a double agent. He couldn't visit Church headquarters anymore because of the GPS system in the chip, and he knew any phone calls or emails would be noticed. So Aaron and his main contact, Elder Benjamin Bushman of the Church's First Quorum of the Seventy, relied on a tried-but-true method to communicate—snail mail.

In ordinary envelopes addressed to each other's wives, they would send coded messages in letters that focused on baking recipes. If someone happened to open the letter they would find three pages filled with tasty tidbits about peach cobbler and apple dumplings. No one would ever suspect that on the back of the pages—written in invisible ink—were Aaron's messages to the Church about the NSA's latest plans.

Elder Bushman would then write him back, giving updates on the Church's preparations in case religious liberties were curtailed by the government. Elder Bushman also often asked specific questions about situations in other parts of the country and whether any of the Church camps needed to be moved to avoid detection, because there had been one "blue camp" in the Midwest that was discovered by the CCA, and the people there had fought back. It had turned into a brutal confrontation that left many people dead.

Afterward, the government leaked a biased report about the incident to the media, saying they had stamped out a group of Mormons who had refused to get the chip. So the Church was now taking even more precautions to avoid similar scenarios.

Aaron sensed that his letters were being read by the Church's First Presidency, and he felt a deep responsibility to share his findings in as much detail as possible. Sometimes his letters were short, but often he would write several pages about ways the Church could stay one step ahead of the government. He knew the prophet had a direct link to the Lord, but he also knew this information was being used by the Church leaders to make crucial decisions that would affect the Saints.

⟨≈⟩

Before leaving work for the day, Aaron decided to risk checking Marie's chip status again. He knew his keystrokes were being monitored, but he just couldn't resist. He had checked Marie's chip status during his lunch break, and everything had been normal. She had still been in her apartment, presumably with Nathan.

As the screen changed to Marie's profile, Aaron let out a gasp. Her chip status had changed to red and blinked "Fugitive." This meant her chip had been removed while she was still alive.

He quickly switched to a different tracking program to check if anyone was in Marie's apartment, and he was shocked to see four individuals on the 26th floor of the Bloomingdale's Building. Judging by their hurried movements from room to room, it was clear they were searching for his daughter.

"Nathan must have cut out her chip to protect her," he whispered. "I hope they're on the run now."

Aaron shut down his computer and hurried to his car. He needed to get home and talk with Carol. He was anxious to tell her the news about Marie, but he didn't want to explain it over the phone. As he came into the house, Carol came to his side.

"Did you see that Chicago's on fire?" she asked. "I'm so worried about Marie. Are you still able to track her?"

"Sort of," he whispered. "I think Nathan cut out her chip today. It looked like people were searching for her."

Carol's knees buckled, and Aaron caught her in his arms. "She'll be okay," he said softly, hoping he was right.

Aaron helped Carol into the living room, where she had been watching the national evening news. A reporter was in a helicopter above Chicago, pointing out the smoke from a massive fire. A strong wind was blowing the smoke east across Lake Michigan, creating an eerie spectacle.

"In just one day, more square miles have burned than in the Great Chicago Fire of 1871," the reporter said. "At the moment, the fire is only 10 percent contained, and a strong wind is pushing the flames directly toward some of the tallest skyscrapers in the world. This could turn out to be an all-time catastrophe."

The screen switched back to the anchorman in the studio. "Do we have any idea how the fire started?"

The reporter shook his head. "Officials are still tight-lipped, but all indications are that this was an act of arson."

Aaron held up his hand. "Hold on! Where's the blame?"

A few seconds later, the anchorman concluded the segment by saying, "Sources indicate that members of a Christian sect are under investigation for causing the blaze."

"Of course," Aaron said tiredly. "It certainly couldn't have been anyone else!"

During the commercial break, Aaron gave Carol more details of what he'd been able to learn about Marie.

"When I saw the men searching the same floor that Marie's apartment is on, I figured they must have detected her chip," Aaron said. "There's a gang leader there named Brix who has teamed up with the government to track everyone down. It was only a matter of time before they found her, whether she was still hiding in the museum or in her apartment. I'm pretty confident that Nathan is with her, and he must've explained that she needed to get rid of the chip."

The news came back on, and an economist was sitting with the anchorman, who said, "I am joined by Dr. Arnold Thompson, who we often consult with on economic matters."

A small inset shot of the burning Chicago skyline was added to the screen as the anchor continued, "Dr. Thompson, we face potentially billions of dollars of damage from this Chicago fire. What will be the immediate impact on the economy?"

Dr. Thompson looked truly irritated. "The president assured us this afternoon that we'll be able to rebuild the Chicago skyline even better than before, but it's time for our nation's leaders to be realistic for once."

"What do you mean?" the anchorman asked, truly surprised at

his guest's comments.

"We're on the verge of hyperinflation," Dr. Thompson said. "Within the past few weeks, oil and other energy prices have climbed. Gasoline is getting harder to come by, and daily expenses are simply too expensive for most families. This fire is going to greatly accelerate all of the misery that many Americans are already going through."

The anchorman clearly didn't expect such an honest assessment. He gave a fake smile to the camera and thanked Dr. Thompson for his comments, then obviously cut the interview short.

Aaron laughed. "It looks like someone is going to get a call from the White House staff tonight. I think the economist was supposed to say how the fire was a blessing, because it was going to create a lot of 'shovel ready' jobs."

Carol didn't find the humor in his statement, partly because she was still sure their house was bugged. She leaned her head on his shoulder, and grasped his hand.

"Aren't you worried about Marie and Nathan?" she asked.

Aaron grew serious. "More than you can imagine."

CHAPTER 7

Over the past three days, Nathan had steadily pushed Marie in the wheelchair through the streets of southern Chicago. They stayed silent, and Marie's sign served as an effective deterrent to keep potential troublemakers away. They had slept the night before under an abandoned school bus, but it hadn't been very restful.

Nathan estimated they had traveled about thirty miles so far, but he also knew that Nauvoo was along the Mississippi River on the western side of Illinois. They were probably still nearly 270 miles away, but he hadn't told Marie that yet.

Throughout the third day they had been traveling south on a road called the Dixie Highway. The area seemed more affluent than those they'd passed through, and on the left side of the road a golf course appeared. A sign on the fence said:

Idlewild Country Club
Flossmoor, Illinois

Marie's eyes lit up. "This place seems nice. Maybe we can find someone here. I'd like to trade some of these cans for something different."

Nathan was definitely getting tired of pork and beans. It was making them both feel sluggish.

"Sounds good," Nathan said. "I really need to take a rest. My whole body aches."

Marie nodded. "You've been pushing yourself too hard. At the very least, maybe we can sleep for a couple of hours."

They walked along the sidewalk for another quarter-mile when they spotted the clubhouse. Marie hopped out of the wheelchair and tried the front door, but it was locked. Nathan pulled Shawn's keys out of his pocket and tried them all, but none of them would open the lock.

"It figures," she said, shaking the door handle a couple more times. Then she noticed an open gate that led to the golf course. "Let's at least go find some shade."

Nathan pushed the wheelchair along a path and followed Marie to a secluded wooded area, where they collapsed on the grass. Before closing his eyes, Nathan peered through the trees, and turned on the chip detector, but he didn't locate anyone nearby. Judging by the length of the grass, no one had been maintaining the golf course for at least a couple of weeks.

He looked over at Marie, who was already drifting off. She was so pretty, but she was also still very frail. He reached over and moved some stray hairs out of her face.

"We just need to get to Nauvoo," Nathan said softly. "Then we'll be able to recover."

⤳

Nathan felt something tapping against his shoulder. He slowly opened his eyes, thinking Marie must be trying to wake him.

"Hold on, Marie," he said. "Just a few more minutes."

"Well, at least we know her name," a deep voice said.

Nathan jerked awake and saw two men in security uniforms staring down at him. The shorter one was pointing a chip detector at Marie, and then he swung it back toward Nathan. He frowned and said, "Hmm. You two have a lot of explaining to do."

Nathan reached over and tugged on Marie's arm. "Hey, wake up. I think we're in trouble."

Marie stirred, then her eyes got big as she saw the men. Nathan helped her stand up.

"A woman reported seeing you trying to get into the clubhouse, so we were sent here to check things out," the taller man said. "Neither of you have a chip, which requires me to turn you into the Chip Compliance Authority."

The other man pointed at Marie's bandaged right hand. "That looks a little fishy. No wonder your chip doesn't register."

Marie stared at him for a moment, then said, "I'm not going to lie. I had the chip, and I cut it out earlier this week, but I only did it because a CCA member had tracked me down and I felt threatened by him. He went way beyond his authority. I was afraid he was going to kill us. Thankfully we got away from him."

"She's right," Nathan said. "We feared for our lives. You two seem much more civilized than that other guy."

The taller man shrugged, slowly pulling a knife out of his pocket. "We hope we're a little gentler out here in the suburbs, but we still need to enforce the law. Besides, you were trespassing on private property. We're going to have to take you into custody and get this sorted out. Follow me."

Nathan motioned for Marie to sit in the wheelchair, and then he pushed her in it, following the taller man toward the clubhouse. The shorter man followed behind them, and Nathan prayed he wouldn't notice the pistol hidden in his waistband.

"We're so sorry," Marie said, on the verge of tears. "Please just let us be on our way."

The men ignored her as they opened the clubhouse and led them into an office, where they motioned toward two folding chairs.

"Stay right there," the taller man said. "We've got a city authority coming to interrogate you."

Meanwhile, Nathan could hear the men checking out the wheelchair in the other room. One man said, "It just looks like pork and beans in this suitcase."

Within two minutes they heard someone else enter the clubhouse.

"Over here," one of the men called out. "They're in the main office."

Nathan and Marie looked nervously at each other as a large middle-aged black man entered the room. He moved behind the desk and slammed his fists down.

"What's your purpose here?" the man shouted, his eyes blazing. "How dare you trespass on this country club! You're lucky someone didn't shoot you!"

Nathan tried to respond, but couldn't get the words out before the man pointed in his face. "Don't say a word. For all I know you're one of those Christians passing through looking for a free handout. You won't find that here!"

He motioned toward Marie. "It looks like you cut your own chip out. I suppose it's just as well, because if you'd had a chip, you never would've made it across our city limits. Our sensors would've been triggered instantly. That's why Flossmoor is still peaceful—we don't let your kind pass through here."

The man paced back and forth, glaring at them. "We ought to just string you up at the city limits as an example of what happens when people don't get the chip."

Marie finally couldn't take it anymore. "Sir, we're from Utah. We've been walking from Chicago for three days. We didn't even know we'd crossed into another city."

Nathan put his hand on her arm, trying to comfort her.

The man stopped in front of Nathan. "Okay. You've got one chance. I want you to tell me exactly why you never got the chip. There's one right answer. Otherwise, we're locking you away."

"Tell the truth," the Spirit prompted.

Nathan's heart began pounding. The truth wasn't what this guy wanted to hear, but he'd take a shot.

"I'm a Christian," Nathan said. "My church leaders counseled us against getting the chip, and I followed that guidance. I believe God doesn't approve of it. The chip limits our freedom, and at this point I'd sacrifice my life before I would get it."

The man stared at Nathan for a full thirty seconds, then he turned to Marie. "What about you? You clearly got it, then cut it out. That's also against the law, you know."

"I made a mistake," Marie said. "I should've never received it, and now I feel the same way about it as Nathan does."

The man frowned at them, his eyes darting back and forth. "So if I took you to a chip implant center right now, you'd choose to die rather than get the chip?"

They both nodded.

"Very well," the man said. "Let's go. We've got an execution chamber at the city hall."

The two other men returned to the room and took hold of them. They forced them back into the clubhouse lobby, where the black man stepped toward them and said, "There's one other thing I need to discuss before you die."

He reached into his pocket and held out an object in front of him. A small metal cross.

Nathan blinked hard, and the black man put his arm around Nathan's shoulder.

"You passed," the man said. "I'm Pastor Haskell, the leader of the local Baptist Church."

Nathan was still unsure what this meant. "So you're not going to lock us up?"

"No, we want you to join us," the pastor said. "Good Christians need to stick together."

Marie let out a sob of relief and collapsed into the wheelchair. "That wasn't nice!" she said. "I nearly had a heart attack."

Pastor Haskell extended his hand to her. "I know. I'm sorry, but we have to be cautious. People will say or do anything right now if they think it will get them some food."

"Where is your group?" Nathan asked. "I hope you aren't planning on staying here too long. I think the mobs aren't far behind us."

"We have a group of about 300 members of my congregation who are going to leave for Springfield," Pastor Haskell said. " We know things in Chicago are getting worse by the day. Did you see a lot of violence on your way here?"

"No but like I said, I think we're just moving ahead of it. We've been trying to stay ahead of the smoke, too. That looks like quite a fire."

"You're right," Pastor Haskell said. "We've been able to get some reports about the situation, and groups of gang members are going into suburban neighborhoods and invading people's homes, where they kill the residents and set the homes on fire. It's only a matter of time before they move south."

"Aren't the police doing anything?" Marie asked. "We haven't seen anyone."

Pastor Haskell shook his head. "The police tried to keep up at first, but there were too many attacks in so many neighborhoods at the same time. Now the residents are fighting back, driving the gangs out and posting roadblocks with armed guards at their neighborhood entrances, but it's just deteriorating into a civil war. I feel the Lord is directing me to lead my congregation to safety while I still can. We have a summer camp near Springfield, and other congregations are going there as well. There will be safety in numbers."

Nathan prayed in his heart and felt the confirmation from the Spirit that they had been led to Pastor Haskell.

"That sounds great," Nathan said. "We'll contribute in every way that we can. You can have all the pork and beans we have."

Pastor Haskell smiled. "We'll take them. That wheelchair will come in handy as well."

By nightfall, Pastor Haskell had taken Nathan and Marie to a small park in a walled community farther south, where members of his congregation were preparing to leave the following day. Pastor Haskell introduced them to several families, and they were warmly welcomed. Among the group were people of seemingly every color and nationality, all working together.

The men in the group had fashioned some contraptions with plywood and bicycle tires that sure looked to Nathan like handcarts. It warmed Nathan's heart to see how the Lord was inspiring Christians of all denominations to take refuge from the coming devastation.

Marie was quickly welcomed by a group of single mothers who were thrilled when she offered to help take care of the kids. One little girl bonded with her immediately, and Nathan smiled as he heard the girl's mother say, "You're a lifesaver, young lady."

At one point, Pastor Haskell was working alongside Nathan, who told him, "I know God helped us find you. Thanks for inviting us."

"You'll be a good addition to our group," Pastor Haskell said. "I'm sorry I had to frighten you that way at the golf course, but I really needed to test your devotion."

"What if we'd said no?" Nathan asked.

"We would've taken you to the police, because you would have shown you couldn't be trusted."

"Did you suspect we were Christians?"

The pastor gave him a small grin. "Your eyes gave you away. A true Christian has a light in his eyes that I've learned to recognize over the years."

"I know what you mean," Nathan said. "I do want you to know we're members of the LDS Church. You know, the Mormons."

Pastor Haskell raised an eyebrow. "Like the Mitt Romney kind of Mormons?"

"Yes."

"All the better," he said. "I used to hate you guys, but before moving here I lived in Long Island, New York, and I saw your members in their yellow shirts helping clean up after Hurricane Sandy."

"You mean the Mormon Helping Hands?" Nathan asked.

"Yeah, that's it. I got to know some of your leaders and they offered my congregation more help than my own leaders did. So now I see we're all on the same team."

As the sun set, Nathan watched a few men carry some crates to the far end of the park. He walked over to Pastor Haskell and asked, "Do they need some help?"

"No, they'd be fine," he said. "Just enjoy the show."

"What show?"

Pastor Haskell gave him a funny look. "Hey, the country might be falling apart, but we're still going to celebrate the Fourth of July."

Nathan felt like he'd been slapped. He hadn't even realized what day it was. "I'm sorry. I didn't mean to be disrespectful. I had honestly lost track of the calendar."

"It's no problem," the pastor said. "We bought these fireworks a few months ago, and since we can't take them with us, we'll start off our journey with a real blast."

Nathan smiled. "Great idea."

A few minutes later he was sitting on the grass next to Marie, who was being climbed on by her new buddy, four-year-old Sylvia.

"We're gonna watch fireworks!" Sylvia shouted, and everyone around them smiled. The fireworks didn't last long, but they were greatly appreciated. The group clapped loudly and then went to bed, planning to arise for a long trek to Springfield that would take several weeks.

Two Months Later

As the "Summer of Discontent" rolled on, new problems seemed to crop up across the United States. Some states were relatively unaffected by the turmoil except for an increase in violent crime and gas shortages, but other areas seemed to get hit repeatedly by those problems, as well as power outages and civil unrest.

A political cartoonist had created a popular drawing entitled "*The State of the Nation*" that symbolized America's turmoil. The drawing showed an American flag unfurled on the ground that had the United States traced on it. The right side of the flag, correlating with the East Coast, was tattered and ragged, with burn marks in trouble spots such as Washington, D.C. and New York City.

The upper center of the flag was completely burned away, symbolizing the upheavals in Chicago and Detroit, while the nation's midsection was frayed and unraveling.

The bottom of the flag was ripped up and covered with dark smudges, showing the remains of Hurricane Barton and the unrest it caused earlier that year.

Then the lower left side looked like a cat with long claws had shredded California into several jumbled strips, symbolizing the results of the massive earthquake and the Black Flu there.

The only part of the flag that was relatively intact was the blue field with the 50 stars, because so far the upper Northwest and other Western states had been fairly unscathed.

However, as the calendar turned to September, that symbolic flag was about to be trampled on by Mother Nature in a way that would affect every single thread.

CHAPTER 8

Garrett Foster gazed out from the Santa Monica Pier and cast his fishing line as far as he could. Then he settled back into the old rocking chair he had pulled out of the surf soon after his arrival.

His life had improved remarkably since he had awakened in that hospital parking lot in Pasadena. He had worried he wasn't even going to make it through that day, but he'd been blessed to reunite with his old military buddy Layne, who had treated him like a long-lost brother.

In the past two months Garrett had established himself as one of the best fishermen, catching several fish each day while getting a good tan. He patted his stomach, which had filled out again thanks to a variety of fish-related meals the women in town created from their daily catches. The widespread bruising and weakness he had suffered from the Black Flu had mostly vanished, and he felt healthier than he had in several years.

The effects of the earthquake were still a part of daily life, but in some ways he felt happier in this new society where material possessions no longer mattered. In the distance he could see large mansions on the hillside that were damaged and uninhabitable, and he thought of all the fancy cars he'd seen abandoned on the freeway. Everyone here was now poor, but there was a steady happiness in their little community.

Some of that tranquility had been shaken two weeks earlier when four men came into Santa Monica and said that electricity had been restored to parts of San Diego and the citizens there were starting to rebuild their society. The men invited the citizens to join them in returning to San Diego and "get back to the way things used to be."

As they told their story, Garrett couldn't resist asking, "How come you're traveling around telling everyone about it? I think I would've kept it a secret for a while."

Their leader smiled. "Well, there are only a few thousand people still alive there, and we need a larger population to really get things rolling again. We need to unite the remaining citizens and establish a functioning society."

The man's answer made sense to a lot of the citizens, and a group of about 100 people said they wanted to go to San Diego. Layne gave them his blessing, and with backpacks over their shoulders they headed off to rebuild civilization.

Garrett considered it briefly, but he'd already seen what was out there, and he doubted very much had changed in that time. This was his reality now, and he had the nagging feeling those men weren't as honorable as they pretended to be. In the back of his mind, he wondered if these citizens were being unknowingly led into some form of slavery. Nothing surprised him anymore.

❦

As he watched the ocean waves roll in, Garrett's thoughts drifted for the thousandth time to his beloved Vanessa. He knew she wouldn't have left him alone at the hospital if she was okay, so he had resigned himself to the fact she was dead. Her body might have been in that same hospital parking lot where he had awakened, but now he'd never know.

He hoped Nathan had somehow reconnected with Denise back in Utah. He still intended to return there if an opportunity presented itself, but right now he was just trying to take life a day at a time.

"Garrett! I think you've got something on the line!" a nearby fisherman called out.

Garrett pulled back on his pole, and sure enough, he'd hooked something fairly big. He stood up and reeled in his line as a few men came to his side.

"Can you see it?" Garrett asked as the line slackened slightly.

A man peered down into the water and smiled. "Yes! It's a nice little shark!"

Garrett decided it would be easier to bring it to shore on the beach, so he hurried along the pier while keeping his line tight. When he reached the beach, a crowd gathered around to watch him reel it in. The shark was strong and kept fighting for nearly twenty minutes, but Garrett was finally able to drag the shark up onto the sand. He collapsed in exhaustion with a big smile on his face as the crowd clapped.

"Nice job," a familiar voice said, and Garrett turned to see Layne walking toward him. "Someone stopped by my office and said you were waging an epic battle down here!"

"Yes, it wore me out," Garrett said as his friend clasped his hand and pulled him to his feet.

Three men dragged the shark over to them. One man said, "It's about six feet long. That's the biggest one we've caught here in a long time."

"Then let's have a celebration," Layne said. "Everyone's invited for a feast at our headquarters tonight!"

⁓

Two hours later, Garrett sat next to Layne at a picnic table in the parking lot outside Layne's office. There were several grills fired up and loaded with the day's catch—including Garrett's shark, of course. The air was filled with delicious aromas as more than 200 people gathered together for the feast.

"This is great," Garrett said. "We never had it this good during the Gulf War."

Layne gave him a wry grin. "Oh, I'm sure you miss those scorching deserts as much as I do."

Garrett noticed Neva approaching, the woman who had

welcomed him to Santa Monica when he first arrived. She was a skilled cook, and she had asked Garrett if she could have the honor of cooking his prized catch. She now carried a plate with two slabs of shark meat and placed it in front of Garrett and Layne.

"I thought I better taste it myself first," she said, pointing to a small corner missing from one of the pieces. "I must say it turned out better than I'd hoped!"

Garrett sliced off a piece and put it in his mouth. He'd never eaten shark meat before, but he was pleased that it tasted like a tangy beef steak.

"Mmmm, this is superb," he said. "Thank you, Neva. Share it with anyone who wants some!"

"I will," she said happily. She returned to her grill, and soon there was a group of people around her waiting for a sample of Garrett's catch.

The other fishermen had also done well that day, and there was plenty of seafood to go around. As they were finishing their meal, Layne said, "Don't go anywhere. I'll be back in a minute."

Garrett watched Layne go into his headquarters and return with his shortwave radio. He sat back down next to Garrett and said, "I didn't want to spoil the party, but I think we might be in for quite a storm tonight."

He pointed to the north, where dark clouds had begun to build. "Those weren't there an hour ago. I was hoping the storm wouldn't ever reach us, but it just keeps coming south."

"How did you find out about it?" Garrett asked.

"My friends up north along the coast have been tracking it for a couple of days. It has really torn things up along through Washington and Oregon. I've been trying to reach my friend in San Francisco, but he isn't responding, which isn't a good sign. I've waited to say anything to the group, but as those clouds get thicker, I think we need to tell everyone."

Layne climbed up on the table and called out, "I hope everyone has enjoyed our feast this evening, but I have something to share with you. Please gather around so you can hear me better."

The group moved toward Layne, and he held up the shortwave radio. "As you know, I've tried to stay in contact with the outside world so we can know if things are improving. Sorry to say, not much has changed, except for the weather."

He motioned toward the thunderheads growing closer from the north. "My friends have let me know that this approaching storm is a terrible one. It has really done a lot of damage up north, with heavy ocean surges and large hailstones. I was hoping it would turn east and miss us, but it looks like we're right in the path. So let's get everything put away, and then we need to move inland and find shelter."

Some of the people nodded, but most of the others looked disinterested, so Layne asked for some feedback.

One man stepped forward. "Sorry, but I've spent all summer getting my place all situated. I'm not going to abandon it. After all we've been through, I think I'll take my chances."

After a few more similar comments, Layne tried to control his frustration. "That's fine, but don't come crying to me when the storm hits," he said. "You've been warned."

෨

Within an hour Layne and Garrett were leading about forty people eastward through the streets of Santa Monica. The rest of the citizens had chosen to stay in their homes near the coast. The dark clouds were now above them, and the wind was blowing inland at nearly forty miles an hour.

By nightfall they came to a large one-story brick home on a small hill. It had some cracks in the walls from the earthquake and had a few broken windows, but Layne said, "This should work. It looks a lot sturdier than the others around here."

The group filed into the home, and soon every room in the house was claimed by various families. Each person had brought a blanket and pillow as part of their supplies, so it soon looked like a huge slumber party throughout the house. Layne had made sure they'd brought candles as well, but the wind was strong enough that it whistled through the broken windows and kept blowing the candles out.

Within minutes, rain began to pelt the house, and the temperature dropped several degrees. Everyone huddled together under their blankets. Layne and Garrett walked through the house to make one final check and saw that every available space was occupied, including the home's two bathtubs.

They returned to the front room and found a spot on the floor. Garrett grabbed his blanket and curled up in a ball, already feeling a bit chilled. "Wake me if you need me," he told Layne, who had settled down next to him.

Layne patted him on the shoulder. "I will, but I doubt we're going to get much sleep tonight."

The house was pitch dark, and everyone was quiet, listening to the high-pitched whistle of the wind as it rushed through the house.

Boom! Boom! Boom!

Garrett sat up in fear as a wave of large hailstones hammered down on the roof. It sounded like a herd of horses was galloping above them. Then a window shattered, followed by another. People shrieked and scurried into other rooms. Some panicked and actually ran outside, where they were struck down and severely injured by the falling ice.

"This is crazy," Layne shouted. He stood up in the darkness, but was unsure how to even respond. "What should we—"

At that moment the front window shattered as a large tree limb crashed through it. Garrett rolled away, receiving only a few scrapes, but the limb caught Layne directly in the chest and drove him into the floor.

"Layne! Layne! Say something," Garrett screamed as he fought through the branches to reach his friend. He reached the limb and felt under it, then recoiled as his hand touched Layne's bloody head. He frantically tried to lift the limb by himself, but it was too heavy.

"Help me," he screamed at the others in the room. "Layne's trapped under the tree."

A few men joined him, and they were able to lift the limb enough to pull Layne out from under it, but Garrett knew it was too late. Even in the darkness it was clear that Layne had sustained a major head injury. Garrett put his head on his friend's chest, but he couldn't hear a heartbeat or detect any breathing.

"No! You can't die!" Garrett shouted. The others moved away back to their own families, allowing Garrett to vent his frustration and grief as he held Layne's body.

❧

The storm continued to beat down relentlessly throughout the night, but Garrett didn't let go of his friend. When morning came, he could see that one of the tree's branches had pierced Layne's neck. He had likely died instantly.

Garrett took a blanket and covered his friend. It was still raining, but the hail had stopped and the winds had died down. He looked around the room, but it was empty. Everyone had moved to other rooms in the house after the tree had crashed through the window.

In despair he threw open the front door to see how extensive the damage was to the area. From the vantage point of the hill, he looked toward the ocean and was shocked to see the streets flooded to within a block of where he stood.

The Santa Monica Pier was gone, and the buildings that had been along the shore were now smashed and strewn everywhere. The damage was so severe that he wondered if a tornado had touched down during the night. He didn't hold out any hope for those who had stayed closer to the shore.

A wave of grief swept through him. This place had helped rejuvenate him, but there was nothing left here for him now. He entered the house again, retrieved a backpack full of food, then stood over Layne's body.

"Thank you, my dear friend. I'll never forget you."

Garrett reached down and touched Layne's face, then he wrapped himself in a blanket and headed south in search of civilization so he could find his children. Nothing else mattered to him now except reuniting with Denise and Nathan.

CHAPTER 9

Aaron Shaw had just stepped out of the shower and was getting dressed when his cell phone rang. He hurried over to his nightstand and grabbed it, hoping not to wake Carol.

"Hello?"

"Hi, Aaron," his supervisor Erik Christensen said. "I just wanted to let you know they've decided to give us the day off. This storm is really causing havoc in California and Nevada, and it's headed our way."

Aaron pulled the bedroom curtain aside and only saw a few clouds in the sky. "The weather looks fine. I shouldn't have any trouble making it to work."

"That's not the issue," Erik said. "The weather service expects it to hit us around noon, so getting home would be the problem. So I'd just stay home and get things tied down. I'll check with you soon to let you know when to come back to work."

"Okay. We'll see how it goes," Aaron said before hanging up.

Carol was now awake. "Are they really expecting the storm to be that bad?" she asked.

"I guess so. Let's see what they're saying on the news."

They went downstairs and settled next to each other on the couch. They turned the TV to the Weather Channel, which was showing a colored graphic of a hurricane-shaped storm more than a thousand miles wide. Over the past two days the center of the storm had traveled south from Washington and Oregon to southern California, and was now pummeling Las Vegas. The outer edges were even affecting Phoenix.

"Whoa, that thing has really grown since last night," Aaron said. "That's impressive."

The screen switched to a series of scenes coming in from Oregon and California showing damaged homes, flooded streets, toppled trees, large hailstones littering the ground, and huge ocean waves crashing onto the shore.

The meteorologist said, "Weather experts are baffled by this storm's unique characteristics. When it formed last week near Russia's eastern coast, there was nothing remarkable about it. Even as it crossed the Pacific and approached Washington state, we expected it to produce moderate rainfall and then fizzle out. Then it started to grow and act like a tropical storm, but what it has done the past two days has never been seen before as it heads west across the Sierra Nevadas."

Carol pointed at the screen as hailstones the size of baseballs were being shown. "Those could kill someone," she said.

They turned the channel to KSL-TV, where the big story was that the edge of the storm had reached the Utah-Nevada border. The first wave of hailstones pulverized the city of Wendover, turning most of the city's neon casino signs into shards of falling glass, killing several people who had taken shelter near the casino entrances.

"The entire state of Utah is vulnerable to hurricane-force winds," the weatherman said. "As this storm approaches, it is vital that you stay indoors."

There was also footage of a long line of 18-wheelers parked along I-80, unable to proceed through the storm. Some had actually blown over, and their cabs and trailers were dented by the hail.

Aaron shook his head. "I can see why they want me to stay home today. I don't want to be out in that!"

The next two hours passed slowly. The weather was perfectly calm with just a few clouds in the sky. Aaron pulled the cars into the garage while Carol and Denise moved throughout the yard, stacking loose items in the garage and then covering their tomato plants with a large tarp.

They continued to look to the western horizon, and a black band of clouds could be seen above the mountains by 11 a.m. Once the storm was in sight, it approached quickly. Aaron called Carol and Denise into the living room, and they kneeled together in prayer. Carol offered to say it.

"Heavenly Father, we ask for thy protection of our home as this storm approaches us. We have sought to do thy will each day, and in our time of need, please spare us from nature's wrath, if it be thy will. We love thee and seek to always serve thee. Please watch over our loved ones as well at this time. In the name of Jesus Christ, Amen."

"Thank you, dear," Aaron said, helping Carol up. "Let me see where the storm is."

He went outside again, and was surprised to see the storm already over Utah Lake. The mountains to the west had vanished behind the approaching black clouds. He hurried back inside and said, "It's nearly here! Let's get ready."

They had already pulled the mattress off their bed and pulled it to the center of the house, where they could take shelter under it if needed.

Thump! Thump! Thump!

The pounding of hailstones could be heard a block away. The severity of the situation became apparent as screams were heard and car alarms were triggered by the storm. The wind was howling and the sunlight disappeared. The power went off, and darkness filled the room. They instinctively got under the mattress.

"I'm scared," Denise cried, cuddling against Carol. Hailstones pounded loudly on the roof, but the windows stayed intact. Fifteen minutes later the pounding stopped, and the commotion seemed to be dying down. Aaron cautiously crept to peer out the front window.

"It's still raining hard, but the hail has stopped," he said. "Come look at this, though. I've never seen such a sight."

They stood at the front window, stunned to see dozens of trees in their neighborhood toppled over, all lying on the ground facing east toward the mountains as if a giant hand had tipped over a row of dominoes.

❧

The power never did come back on in Orem that day, but the clouds seemed to lighten as the rain decreased to a steady drizzle. Aaron ventured out in the evening to see how the house had fared. The roof's shingles were shredded, but overall the roof looked okay. The trees in the yard were badly damaged by the hail, with several broken limbs.

As Aaron looked at other homes along their street, he knew Carol's heartfelt prayer had been answered. Some houses had gaping holes in the roofs and shattered windows. Two houses on the next block had their roofs lifted completely off and scattered across several yards.

When Aaron finally returned home and told Carol and Denise what he had seen, they both expressed relief that their home had been relatively spared.

"The Lord has blessed us," Denise said, putting her arms around Carol.

"Yes, he has," Carol responded. "Tomorrow we'll see how we can help our neighbors."

CHAPTER 10

Nathan smiled with admiration as he watched Marie carrying her young friend Sylvia on her back near the pond in their camp. Pastor Haskell was standing nearby.

"I'm quite impressed with Marie," he said. "You better not let her get away."

Nathan smiled. "Yeah, I'm hoping things work out for us."

Pastor Haskell shook his head. "What are you waiting for? I've got the authority to get you two hitched right now."

Nathan rolled his eyes. "I haven't even proposed . . ."

"I know, I know," the pastor said with a chuckle. "You're waiting until you get back with your family. I still think you're crazy for waiting, though."

Nathan waved him off good-naturedly, and then headed toward Marie. He and Pastor Haskell had become close friends over the past two months as they had traveled with the pastor's congregation to Lake Springfield Baptist Camp near Springfield, Illinois. It had taken the group from the Fourth of July until the week after Labor Day to walk the 200 miles from Chicago, but they'd made it with only two deaths—an infant and an elderly man.

The camp was situated in a beautiful wooded area on the shore of Lake Springfield. The camp would typically be filled with youth groups at this time of year, but now it had become a gathering place for several Baptist congregations. Pastor Haskell's group had arrived three days earlier, and the people who were already there had welcomed them graciously.

As Nathan approached Marie, his heart started beating just a little faster. He had admired her for years, but since the day he'd rescued her from the museum in downtown Chicago, she had taken huge leaps in her maturity and priorities. She hadn't worn makeup in more than two months, but Nathan thought she was more beautiful than ever before. Now that they'd lost all of their material possessions—including the cell phone that had been seemingly attached to Marie's left hand— she had blossomed into a true Saint. She had helped Sylvia's mother with her children every day of the journey, and the kids even called her Aunt Marie.

As Nathan reached them, Marie and Sylvia were crouched down watching a little watersnake squirm across the trail.

"It looks like you two are having fun," Nathan said.

Marie jumped up with a startled look on her face. "You scared me!" she said. "You know I get jittery around snakes—even when they're cute and little."

The snake slithered into the tall grass next to the pond and quickly vanished.

"That's okay," Sylvia said. "We'll catch another one soon, right Aunt Marie?"

"Yep, we'll search in this same place later," Marie said. "But it's almost lunchtime."

"That's right," Nathan said. "Let's join the others."

Nathan had worried how everyone in such a large group would stay fed, but so far that hadn't been a problem. The camp supervisors had already been raising rabbits as part of the camp's summer youth program, and now they purposely let them reproduce as often as possible. This provided a seemingly endless supply of meat. Marie had struggled with the meal on the first night, having had a pet bunny as a girl, but now she savored every bite.

They all ate under a large pavilion, and Pastor Haskell always began each meal with a few jokes, and then a blessing on the food. Today, however, he looked solemn as he stood before them. He wasn't the jovial man that Nathan had joked with just a few minutes earlier.

"My dear brothers and sisters, I've just been informed that three members of the Talley family have come down with symptoms of the Black Flu. The whole family has been quarantined in a cabin on the far end of the camp. If you've been near the members of the Talley family in the past couple of days, you must receive an exam from one of the camp nurses. Hopefully we can nip this outbreak in the bud before anyone else is affected."

"I was hoping the flu had faded away," Nathan whispered to Marie. "At least we haven't been with the Talleys. I'm not sure I could even tell you who they are."

Marie looked at the ground. "I could. They're Sylvia's cousins. I was with them yesterday."

⌇

Within ten minutes, Nathan's world had turned upside down. He had gone with Marie to visit the nurse, who immediately pointed out some dark colorations on Marie's arms. "I'm sorry," she said, "but it doesn't look good."

"Are you sure those aren't just regular bruises?" Nathan asked. "Marie, you were carrying Sylvia around all day."

"I'm sure," Marie said in a trembling voice. "We need to have Sylvia checked as well."

The nurse checked Nathan just in case, but he didn't show any symptoms. An hour later, nearly twenty people—including Marie and Sylvia—were escorted to the quarantined area. Nathan stayed with her, despite the chance of being infected.

"Pray for me," Marie told Nathan as she entered an area of the camp that had been roped off and marked with homemade "Danger" signs.

"I will," he said sadly. "We've come too far together for it to end this way."

"Maybe," she said. "I'm ready to meet my Maker, though."

"Don't talk that way," Nathan cried. "I love you."

"I love you, too."

Then she turned toward the cabin. As Nathan watched her

walk away, he felt like he'd been kicked in the stomach. He knew it wasn't rational thinking, but he wished he'd contracted the illness as well, because he could hardly stand the thought of being away from her again.

Once Marie was inside the cabin, Nathan walked slowly back to find Pastor Haskell, hoping for some sympathy. However, as he returned to the main pavilion, everyone was looking toward the west. It was early afternoon, but the sun had suddenly disappeared behind a wall of dark clouds. It almost felt like a solar eclipse, except for the continual stream of lightning flashes filling the entire horizon. Nathan found the pastor standing in the pavilion speaking to several men.

"We need to get everyone into the meeting halls before it gets here," Pastor Haskell told them. "I don't think the tents are going to hold up."

The camp had three large meeting halls for groups up to 100 people, so it would be a tight squeeze for the camp's 400 occupants to fit, but by the time the storm started pounding the camp just after 2 p.m., everyone was safely inside one of the halls. Nathan was grateful for the small blessing that each of the buildings had restrooms, and even though the power was out, the toilets still flushed.

❧

Amazingly, the storm hadn't lost any of the ferocity that it had shown in California and Utah. If anything, it had picked up steam again. It had merged with a tropical storm that had just crossed the Gulf of Mexico, giving the main storm a supercharge of moisture as it headed toward the East Coast.

Nathan was stationed at the front door of one of the halls. His purpose was to encourage everyone to stay inside, even though it wasn't too difficult once the baseball-sized hailstones started bouncing off the ground and thundering on the roof.

"Look at the size of those things," an awestruck woman said, peering past him out the door's window. "Unbelievable!"

The buildings were sturdy and held up well under the onslaught of wind and hail. Only a couple of windows shattered, and they were able to prop tables against the openings. It was a frightening afternoon, but everyone stayed dry.

As night fell, people tried to lay down, but there wasn't room for everyone at once, so most of the men stood for most of the night while the women and children slept.

By morning the worst of the storm had passed, but the camp's beautiful landscape had suffered. Dozens of trees had been uprooted and now blocked the roads and paths. It would take weeks to clean up. The tents had blown away, except for a few which were now in the tops of nearby trees.

The people were exhausted from being packed like sardines all night, so even though there was still a steady rain, most of them went outside and started the cleanup process, while several women went to the pavilion to try cooking breakfast.

Nathan's first stop was to help salvage anything from the camp's garden. Due to the dire economic conditions, the camp's residents had planted a large garden earlier that year filled with corn, tomatoes, and other vegetables. However, the hailstones had demolished everything. They would be able to save some of the tomatoes and ears of corn, but the plants themselves looked like someone had smashed them mercilessly to the ground.

As Nathan stood at the edge of the garden, the scripture in Doctrine and Covenants 29:16 came to his mind. The verse had always intrigued him, because he had wondered how it could be fulfilled. Now he had his answer as he muttered, *"And there shall be a great hailstorm sent forth to destroy the crops of the earth."*

◦✿◦

Although Marie was constantly in his thoughts, Nathan was so busy helping families get organized that it wasn't until the next day that he had a chance to return to the quarantined area.

As he approached that area, he was shocked to see Pastor Haskell stepping out of one of the cabins. He hadn't seen the pastor since the storm had begun, but even from a distance he could tell Pastor Haskell had caught the Black Flu. The pastor spotted Nathan and turned toward him.

"Stay back, Nathan," the pastor said. "I made the mistake of checking on them yesterday, and I've caught the disease. That's how contagious this new strain is. You need to stay strong for the others. I hope to fight this off and rejoin you."

"How is Marie?" Nathan asked. "I want to see her."

The pastor's shoulders slumped. "She's resting now. Maybe you can see her later."

"She's dying, isn't she?" Nathan cried, and the pastor looked away. "I need to see her."

"Yes, go to her side," a voice said.

Nathan knew that voice, and without hesitation he leapt over the rope that marked the quarantined area and ran toward the cabin he'd seen Marie go into two days earlier.

Pastor Haskell shouted, "Nathan! Don't do it!"

Nathan ignored him and pulled the door open. On a bed in the far corner of the room he saw Marie and Sylvia laying side by side. Sylvia was weeping on Marie's shoulder, but Marie was staring blankly ahead, her chest heaving slowly.

"Nathan, she's not breathing very good," Sylvia said. "I'm so scared."

Nathan moved closer and was stunned to see Marie's face and arms covered with purple pimples. Some had popped and were oozing onto the blanket. Pastor Haskell had entered the cabin and sadly shook his head at Marie's condition.

"This is terrible," Nathan said to him, thinking it might be best for Marie if she passed away. Even if she recovered, her mind might never be the same. He could barely resist caressing her face, though, and moved his hand toward her.

"Don't touch her!" the pastor cried. "The nurses say this new round of the disease has mutated into something even more sinister.

The pus in those pimples is highly contagious. I think it's going to get us all this time."

"Oh, Marie," Nathan cried, shaking his head in grief.

"Use your priesthood, and let the power of God be manifest."

The words struck his heart. He immediately placed his hands on Marie's head and said, "Marie Shaw, in the name of Jesus Christ and by the power of the Holy Melchizedek Priesthood I hold, I command you to be made whole in body and spirit. I command the illness that afflicts you to depart! Be healed!"

Nathan backed away, and Marie's body convulsed three times as if she'd been shocked with a jolt of electricity. Then she gave a loud moan and opened her eyes. She glanced at Nathan, then they all stared in amazement as the pimples on her arms appeared to dry up and flake away, leaving clear pink skin. The pimples on her face did the same thing.

"Praise the Lord," Pastor Haskell said, trying to comprehend what he had just seen. The others in the room gasped in surprise.

Nathan extended his hand to Marie, who slipped her legs over the side of the bed and slowly stood up to embrace him.

"It's not your time to go to the Spirit World," Nathan said softly. "You still have work to do here."

"Good," Marie said. "I was so worried until you came. I couldn't catch my breath. My lungs were filled with fluid. Now I feel better than I have in weeks."

Suddenly Nathan received another prompting.

"Give blessings to the others in the cabin. The Lord wants them to be preserved as well. Then your work among this people is finished and you must move on to Nauvoo."

Nathan looked at Pastor Haskell. "I hold the priesthood of God and have been blessed with the gift of healing. Do you have faith that God can heal you?"

The pastor nodded humbly. "I do."

He sat on the side of the bed, and Nathan blessed him using the same words he'd used in Marie's blessing. The pimples began drying up before Nathan was even finished.

"It's a miracle!" the pastor shouted as he looked at his hands and arms. "God is with you!"

Nathan then followed the prompting he'd received and blessed everyone in the quarantine cabins, beginning with little Sylvia, who immediately leaped off the bed after her blessing.

It took Nathan about twenty minutes to move among the afflicted people and heal them. The Spirit was nearly overpowering, and several people were openly weeping with joy as they and their loved ones hugged each other.

Toward the end, Nathan reached a woman named Velma who had become notorious during their journey for being mean-spirited. She had even criticized Nathan and Marie for various things, and as Nathan stood before her, he naturally hesitated.

"Move on," Velma said. "I know I don't deserve it."

"Do you believe in God?" Nathan asked her.

"I do," she said, starting to weep.

"Then trust in the Lord," he said as he placed his hands on her head. "Velma, by the power of the holy Melchizedek Priesthood, I command this illness to leave your body so that you may be made whole. I also bless your spirit that you may have a change of heart, and look at the positive side of life. The Lord loves you and wants you to reach out to others with good works. If you do so, your life will be spared for many years to come. I leave this blessing upon you in the name of Jesus Christ, Amen."

Velma's eyes suddenly filled with light, and the pimples on her body faded away. She reached up and embraced Nathan.

"I will," she said through her tears. "I will!"

❧

Once all of the blessings were concluded, Pastor Haskell clasped Nathan on the shoulder. "We need to share what has happened with everyone in the camp. Let's return to the pavilion and rejoice in the miracles we've seen."

Nathan turned to Pastor Haskell. "You've been so good to us, but Marie and I need to move on. The Lord has other work for us to do."

Pastor Haskell was surprised, but then he nodded slowly. "Yes, there are many others who need you, but at least let us give you enough provisions for your journey."

"That would be nice," Nathan said. "Thank you."

By the time Nathan and Marie reached the pavilion, the others who were healed had spread the word about what happened. The wheelchair that Marie had used to escape from Chicago had been used by several ailing members of the group throughout the journey. Now it was loaded with a variety of canned foods, but at Marie's request, there weren't any pork and beans included.

Marie and Nathan couldn't withhold their tears as Pastor Haskell said, "We'll never forget what you've done for us."

"It wasn't me," Nathan said. "The Lord deserves all of the credit."

Pastor Haskell gave them some maps of Illinois, and they were able to plot a course along several rural roads to Nauvoo. They estimated the city was about 150 miles away, and they hoped to get there in less than two weeks if they could set a good pace.

Within the hour they were on their way down the road. As Nathan pushed the loaded wheelchair, Marie practically skipped alongside him, thrilled to be healed and headed toward Nauvoo.

"I can't wait to be with the Saints again," Marie said.

Nathan smiled to himself, grateful to hear her say those words.

CHAPTER 11

The following Sunday, Aaron Shaw arrived at a meetinghouse in north Orem a few minutes before Sacrament Meeting was scheduled to begin. He was on Church business, keeping tabs on the Saints who hadn't accepted the prophet's invitation to gather to the mountain camps.

As members began entering the chapel, Aaron was approached by Brother Thomas, a former Elders Quorum president.

"Brother Shaw, it's so good to see you," Brother Thomas said. "Are you here on stake business today?"

Aaron had served for several years on the Stake High Council, and many members of this ward remembered him in that role, so he played along with it.

"Yes," Aaron said. "I wanted to see how your ward members had survived the storm. Who is presiding today?"

"I am," the man said. "We've started rotating the assignment among the brethren in the ward—just until the bishop gets back, of course. I'd be honored if you'd sit on the stand with me."

"Thank you. I'd like that."

Aaron knew the General Authorities truly were still concerned about these Church members who had stayed behind in the valleys, but they couldn't force them to be obedient. So the Church had asked men such as Aaron who were in "double agent" roles to visit wards and report on anyone who was asserting unrighteous dominion or were trying to develop a following as a prophet. In those cases, the Church would send a representative to renounce him and set things in order.

Fortunately for Aaron, the wards he had visited were actually functioning fairly close to how they had before. The bishops of nearly every ward had gathered to the mountain camps, but most wards had at least one key priesthood leader who had stayed behind, and that man usually had taken the reins of the ward.

Several years earlier, Aaron had been in a ward where the bishop had been out of town for six straight weeks, and during that time the ward had felt out of sync and disjointed. These wards now had that same feeling, where the three-hour block of meetings went forward, but nothing of substance really got done.

He and Carol had been attending their old ward for Denise's sake, because she truly did seem interested in the Church, but it did test their patience a bit. They sometimes had to remind each other that the strongest Saints were now tucked away in the mountains, preparing to build Zion.

Aaron also noted that the members who hadn't gathered with the Saints were typically the ones who had always considered themselves "active" by simply showing up on Sunday to sit through Sacrament Meeting and maybe one other class. They had rarely participated in preparing the lessons or teaching the classes, so for these people, they didn't sense much change in the usual routine. They had continued to attend church week after week as if nothing had changed, other than the fact all those "wackos" in the ward had gone to the mountains.

Aaron tried not to judge the remaining ward members. There had been a sifting of the Saints when each person had made their choice whether to follow the prophet. The ones who remained in the valleys simply weren't spiritually prepared to leave everything behind for the gospel's sake. Aaron realized if they'd gone to the camps, they would have been a drain on the resources, talents and morale of those who had heeded the prophet's invitation.

Aaron liked sitting on the stand so that he could see the current demographics of the ward. By the time the meeting started, there were only about 40 people in the pews—several older ladies, some middle-aged couples, and only a few young people and children.

After the opening hymn and prayer, Brother Thomas stood at the pulpit and said, "I've been pondering all morning about what topic to speak on today, and then I saw High Councilman Shaw at the back of the chapel. He's here to find out how our ward dealt with the big storm. So even though it isn't Testimony Meeting this week, I feel prompted to open the meeting for you to share your experiences."

Aaron nodded, pretending as if this was perfectly normal, before stealing a glance toward the empty Sacrament table. Once Brother Thomas was back in his seat, Aaron nudged him and whispered, "What about the Sacrament?"

"We only do that once a month now," he said. "It still counts the same, right?"

Aaron was stunned at the response. He was even more surprised when for the next hour a dozen members came to the pulpit to complain about how the Church and the government hadn't helped them in their time of need. Only two people expressed gratitude for the gospel, but then they also complained about one thing or another.

By the end of the meeting Aaron's heart ached. He knew these were good people, but for various reasons—a lack of faith, attachment to their material possessions, or just fear of change— they had chosen to not follow the prophet, and it was evident that the Spirit wasn't present in the meeting.

Aaron thought about the "spiral dream" that Nathan had once shared with him, where the Saints either had to rise to another level, or they would inevitably slip lower. He realized he was witnessing that happening among these members, and they faced a long hard climb if any of them were going to ever reach that top level of spirituality.

The meeting ended, and Aaron shook hands with several of the members. He liked mingling with them, but he also felt like grabbing them by the shoulders and saying, "There's no time to waste! The government is tracking everything you do. They know you're all here, and they could round you up and put you in a concentration camp before you even knew what hit you! Find your way to the Wallsburg camp before it's too late!"

But he knew that it wouldn't make a difference at this point— they simply weren't listening to the Spirit anymore. As he got in his car and headed home, the words the Savior spoke to the wicked Nephites in Third Nephi 10 came into his mind: "How oft would I have gathered you as a hen gathereth her chickens, and ye would not."

Aaron still felt the Lord was reaching out to them even now, because after Nathan had led the group up Provo Canyon to the Wallsburg camp, the word spread that the option was available. Yet these members didn't feel compelled to leave the comfort of their homes. They all acted like the recent storm was the worst thing they'd ever have to encounter, but Aaron sensed something else was coming soon that would make them barely remember it.

He returned home and wrote to Elder Bushman about the Saints' attitudes and actions, and he promised to report soon on how the government intended to respond to the recent storm.

❧

Aaron returned to work the next day for the first time since the storm had hit Utah. The storm had just finished its path of destruction across the United States by smashing most of the East Coast before heading out into the Atlantic Ocean.

With the East Coast in shambles, Aaron's first assignment was to help the government track the movements of citizens in several communities near Charlotte, North Carolina, which had suffered a direct hit. He immediately noticed thousands of people clustering around federal buildings in search of government assistance. There was already indications of violence and civil unrest in those areas, because hundreds of the implanted chips he was tracking had changed to "Asleep" in just the past two hours. He signaled his supervisor, Erik, who came over to his desk.

"We need to alert the officials that deadly riots are taking place in Charlotte," Aaron said.

Erik merely nodded and jotted down the information.

"You don't seem too concerned," Aaron said. "They need to send in the National Guard immediately to check it out."

Erik shrugged. "I'll report it, but there are at least twenty other cities in worse shape right now. We're hoping the local officials can get things under control."

Aaron sighed. "I wouldn't bet on it."

Their conversation was interrupted by an announcement over the speaker system. "*We've received word that the president is going to speak to the nation in ten minutes. It is mandatory viewing for every NSA employee. Please be seated in the main conference room before that time.*"

Aaron frowned and exchanged a frustrated glance with Erik. These mandatory meetings usually led to a lot more work for both of them.

"Well, I'll see you there," Erik said before walking away.

Aaron took a couple of minutes to save the data he'd been compiling, then he joined his co-workers in the conference room. On a large screen was an image of a podium with the White House logo behind it. Within seconds, the president emerged and stepped to the podium. Aaron noticed how gray the president's hair had turned in the past few years, and that his once-youthful smile and mannerisms had faded into a fairly constant scowl. Today, though, he flashed a grin at the camera.

"My fellow Americans, Mother Nature has given us quite a lashing this past week, but we shall rise above it. I have already authorized FEMA to provide full assistance in more than 30 states that were affected by the storm."

The president looked down briefly at his notes, then continued, "I have also been in constant communication with our medical experts throughout the country, and they say that a new strain of the Black Flu has surfaced. It appears to be more contagious and deadly than the first wave that we dealt with. In response to the combination of the storm's devastation and the return of the illness, I have consulted with our friends at the United Nations during this time of need. They have kindly agreed to send a large contingent of peacekeepers to assist us in rebuilding our cities and to help us control any lawlessness that might take place. They will be bringing much-needed supplies of food, since the storm has left much of our country's autumn crop in ruins."

Aaron could hardly believe his ears. Yes, the United States was currently in bad shape, but having U.N. forces on American soil wasn't going to go over well with Middle America.

The president seemed to realize what his announcement might spark, because he quickly added, "I repeat, they are coming to help us. Please don't treat them like an invading army or engage in any type of violence toward them. Follow their instructions and you'll find safety. Many of them will speak another language, but I assure you that in their hearts they only seek the same thing we all do— world peace."

Aaron actually dug his fingernails into his palms to make sure he wasn't dreaming. He asked himself, "Did the U.S. president really just instruct his fellow countrymen to follow the orders of U.N. forces? What's next? Martial law?"

As if on cue, the president got a pained look on his face. "Over the past few days, I have struggled to find the best way that can get our country back on track and stop the growing violence on our streets. Finally one choice emerged as the best direction for the nation. For a very limited time, I am now enacting what is known as martial law. Large gatherings will be prohibited in order to curtail the flu and to avoid dangerous situations. This will protect our law-abiding citizens from those who seek to do harm. Combined with the help we'll receive from our U.N. friends, I expect things will turn around quickly. My goal is that by Thanksgiving Day, we will have much to celebrate. These troubles will be behind us, and a new era of prosperity will begin. Thank you."

The president stepped away from the podium and quickly disappeared from the screen. Aaron looked around the room at dozens of people who had supported this president for years. He thought he might hear some comments in defense of the president, but everyone sat motionless for several seconds, as if a truth had finally dawned on them—the kind of positive change they'd been expecting was never going to come.

Aaron returned to his desk and saw he'd missed a call from Carol. He called her back, and her first words were, "I think Denise and I need to go camping really soon."

Aaron felt a wave of relief. "I was thinking the same thing."

CHAPTER 12

A few days later in California, Garrett Foster walked along the Pacific Coast Highway. He was heading south in hopes of finding the group that claimed they had electricity again. It was a long walk to San Diego, but after seeing his friend Layne killed, he just couldn't stay in Santa Monica anymore. He knew he was going though some form of depression, but he couldn't shake it. Everything seemed to be combining against him.

He was currently passing through Long Beach, California. He hadn't encountered anyone else for two days, but as he climbed an overpass and looked toward the ocean, he was shocked to see vehicles driving around. He left the highway and cautiously walked along a street toward the ocean. Along the way, he saw signs with directions to the Port of Los Angeles.

He was soon close enough to the port that he could see dozens of men who seemed to be speaking Russian to each other. They were methodically unloading a wide variety of equipment onto a dock from several huge ships. They had already unloaded dozens of large, strange-looking trucks, which were now parked in long rows. Some of the trucks had four or five drive axles and looked too wide to drive down a single lane of a highway. The trucks were loaded with a great deal of cargo, such as food, medical supplies, fuel, and other necessities.

He pondered what these vehicles could possibly be for, and he realized they could be very useful in traveling on damaged roads. One of these trucks could cross a ten-foot-wide crevasse and the passengers wouldn't even notice.

He crouched next to a building and watched them for a few minutes, wondering if America had been invaded, but he hadn't heard any explosions, and no one seemed to be in a big hurry to finish their tasks.

A jeep suddenly turned onto the street heading toward him, and he ducked around the corner as it passed by. There were two men in the jeep, and they definitely weren't American soldiers. They appeared to be Asian and were wearing blue helmets.

He continued to watch the men on the dock and somehow didn't hear the jeep slowly circle back toward him. Before Garrett could react, a man jumped out of the jeep with a pistol in one hand and some sort of device in the other.

"Don't move, Garrett Foster," the man said. "You're now in the custody of the United Nations."

Garret raised his hands above his head. "How did you know my name?"

The man glanced down at the device he was holding. "Your chip, of course. We aren't going to harm you, but we're taking you in for questioning."

❧

Garrett was soon standing under a pavilion in a Long Beach park with 50 other people who had been rounded up that morning. They were all handcuffed, and he knew trying to escape would be fruitless. There were several more men than women in the group, but the women looked more hardened and angry, as if they were ready to kill someone—and probably already had.

Garrett had been treated kindly so far by the U.N. guards, but he noticed some of the other detainees were kept away from the others. They seemed genuinely insane, talking to themselves and randomly shouting at the guards.

Three Asian men carrying laptop computers entered the pavilion and took seats at a table. They wore distinctive uniforms emblazoned with the U.N. insignia. They opened their laptops, and the one in the center motioned to the guards standing next to the handcuffed detainees.

"Let's get them out of the way," he said in perfect English. "They're probably part of that same group we dealt with yesterday who lived in that care center down the road."

As the first man was led before them, the U.N. official on the left ran a chip scanner over the man's right hand.

"Yep," the middle official said, looking at the laptop screen. "His last residence was the Long Beach Mental Health Center. Take him away."

The next five men were also from the same facility, then came one of the women who had made Garrett nervous. After her chip was scanned, the lead official smiled a little. "Hmm. Your last occupation was as a dancer for the Los Angeles Lakers?"

"That's right," she said. "You got a problem with that?"

"No," he said. "I just don't quite know where you'll fit into our new society. The records show you were divorced twice, and have lived off food stamps for the past five years. That's not very productive."

The woman started to cry. "Please don't judge me. I can do anything—cook, clean, sweep . . ."

The leader paused, then shook his head. "I think we need to evaluate you more. Take her with the others."

"No! Give me a chance," she cried out as the guards seized her and took her to the same building where the others had gone.

Most of the interviews were short, because admittedly the ones they'd rounded up that day were homeless people before the earthquake and had simply never left the downtown area.

After each person was questioned, he or she was escorted toward one of two buildings. So far, Garrett had seen nearly two dozen people escorted to the building on the left where the insane ones had been taken. Only two people, a man and a woman, had been taken to the building on the right. Both had seemed more "normal" than the rest of the group. The man had been a mechanic, while the woman could speak several languages.

Garrett looked down at his dirty clothes and ran his fingers through his growing beard. He felt as if he were about to have a major job interview but had forgotten to bathe ahead of time. All he knew was he wanted to be led to the building on the right where the few competent people had gone.

Finally Garrett was led in front of the U.N. officials, and after his chip was scanned, the leader spent a full minute reading through the data on his screen.

"Well, Corporal Foster, it's safe to say you probably feel a little out of place here," he said, motioning to the other people.

"I suppose," Garrett said.

"Why didn't you just say you had military experience when they picked you up?" the U.N. official asked. "Serving in the Gulf War would have been worth mentioning. We could've spared you these indignities."

Garrett shrugged. "I've been stuck in Santa Monica for nearly three months without electricity, so I'm not quite sure what is going on here. Has America been invaded?"

The U.N. leader grinned. "No, we're part of the U.N. forces who are here to help America get back on its feet. Your country has always been generous to the rest of the world in giving disaster aid, and now it's our turn to respond."

Garrett breathed a sigh of relief. "As an American soldier, where do I fit in?"

"We can certainly use your expertise as our peacekeepers move forward throughout this region. You'll be a valuable resource in suggesting areas we should repair."

"That sounds great," Garrett said.

The leader glanced again at the screen. It says you've been living in Orem, Utah. Is that near Salt Lake City?"

"About forty miles away."

"Excellent," the leader said. "I know our overall plans include traveling there soon. You could be part of our advance team."

"It would be my privilege," Garrett said, happy to have found a way back to Denise.

The leader pointed toward the building on the right. "Now go take a shower, get cleaned up, and fill your stomach. There's plenty of work to do!"

"Yes sir!" Garrett said with a smile before breaking into a trot toward the building. Life suddenly seemed worth living again.

CHAPTER 13

Aaron and Carol had spent the last week figuring out a way for she and Denise to escape to one of the mountain camps. Orem had quickly become a dangerous place to be at night, and they were going to use that to their advantage.

They had to talk in code, since they were still worried their house was bugged, and finally Aaron wrote down a step-by-step list of how they could pull it off. Carol read through it and nodded, although it was more dangerous than she had expected.

"They have to think you're dead," Aaron whispered. "Otherwise they'll lock me up and hunt you down."

Aaron wished they hadn't waited so long to send Carol and Denise to a Church camp. They had always planned to go, and Carol knew the password needed to enter the best camps, but they had held off so that they could stay together as long as possible. Plus, there was always the slim hope that Marie would show up on their doorstep.

However, the president's proclamation of Martial Law had changed everything. Now the employees of the Chip Compliance Authority were allowed to essentially work without restraint, especially when it came to any reports of unauthorized chip removal.

When a so-called "fugitive" was caught, it was an automatic six-month prison sentence—if the CCA enforcers didn't "accidentally" kill the person while transporting them to prison. Aaron was sickened by the number of times he'd had to categorize a death as RADT, meaning "Resisted Arrest During Transport."

They had kept Denise in the dark about what was going to happen, although she might inadvertently ruin the plan if she didn't know the details. It was a risk they were prepared to take, because one slip of her tongue might send the CCA rushing to their home.

The evening had finally come. As Denise finished her dinner, Aaron and Carol went into the bedroom, where they knelt down and Aaron whispered, "Dear Father, we feel it is time for Carol and Denise to join the other Saints in the mountains so they can be protected from the troubles that are coming and help build Zion. Please be with them as they travel, and guide them during their journey. Please allow our plan to proceed. In the name of Jesus Christ, Amen."

They returned to the dining room, and Carol asked, "Denise, why don't we go to Target? I've been wanting to buy you that new dress you tried on the last time we were there."

"Really? That would be great," Denise said, smiling widely.

"I'll see you later," Aaron said. "I'm going to stay here and clean up the kitchen while you're gone. Have fun!"

Carol and Denise went to the garage and got in the car, and soon they were in the Target parking lot. Carol parked farther from the store than she needed to, away from any other vehicles.

"Why don't you take one of the closer stalls?" Denise asked.

"This will be fine," Carol said. "I could use the walk."

They went inside, and while Denise searched for the dress she'd wanted, Carol breathed in her surroundings. She was eager to go to the camp and rejoin the Saints, but she was admittedly going to miss everyday modern life. However, it was clear things weren't normal. Even in the past couple of weeks, the shelves were only partially filled, as if they weren't being restocked. She realized Utah had been spared much of the turmoil that was taking place elsewhere in the country, but it was starting to affect everyday life even in Orem.

"I found it!" Denise called out. "I was starting to worry someone else had bought it."

Carol turned to see Denise holding the dress in front of her. "Yes, that's the one. It will look nice on you."

At the checkout stand, Carol made sure to use her chip to verify that she had been there. "Hold on," she said to the cashier as she grabbed two Snickers bars from a nearby display. "Add these to my bill."

As they walked back to the car, Carol handed Denise one of the candy bars. "I thought we deserved a little treat."

As they approached the car, Carol's nerves started to get to her. This was the part of the plan she had dreaded the most. She finished her candy bar, then turned to Denise while they still stood in the parking lot, since she was sure the car was bugged as well.

"This is a very important night," Carol said. "You and I have a special trip. Have we told you very much about the camps in the mountains where some of the Mormons have gone?"

"A little. Isn't that what Nathan was helping with?"

"That's right. He was taking food to the camps so that everyone there would have enough to eat. I think it would be great to live there. It certainly isn't as dangerous as it is here."

Denise nodded. "You know what? I want to go to the camps. Do you think that's where Nathan and Marie are going?"

"That's what Aaron says," Carol said. "I really want to see them again. I'm afraid if we stay here, we never will."

"Then why don't we just go?" Denise asked.

Carol shook her head. "Aaron can't leave his job right now. It would have to just be the two of us."

"We could make it," Denise said. "Let's go."

Carol kept shaking her head. "We have the chip implant, and they won't let us into the camp with one. Plus, the CCA would track us down."

Denise sat silently for a moment, then said, "I'm willing to cut mine out. I've been wanting to for a long time."

Carol was surprised. She was wondering how she was ever going to convince Denise to cut out her chip, but she'd already come up with the idea herself.

"It will hurt, but I'm willing to do it if you are," Carol said. "I can get out the First Aid kit."

Denise's eyes got wide as she realized Carol was serious, but then she pursed her lips. "Yes, let's do it."

Carol opened the car trunk where she had put the First Aid kit. The trunk had a small light that shined just enough so she could see what she was doing. She wasted little time cutting out her own chip, and Denise helped apply a bandage before it bled very much. Then it was Denise's turn, and she handled it bravely. Carol deliberately tossed the chips under the car and said, "We need to go now."

"Can't we drive there?" Denise asked.

"No, we'd never make it to our destination without getting stopped," Carol replied, "so we'll be walking."

She reached into the trunk again and grabbed two backpacks she had prepared the night before that were filled with water, food, and other essentials. She tried not to draw attention to the four gas cans stashed in the trunk as well. She handed a backpack to Denise and said, "Make sure you put that nice dress in your pack."

After Denise had done so, Carol put her arm around Denise and started walking rapidly toward Orem's Center Street. She hoped they could make it the few miles to Provo Canyon before resting.

When they were about a block away, Carol said, "There's just one more thing to do." She pulled a small box from her pocket and opened it up. Inside was a remote control pad. She entered a few digits, then confidently pressed a red button.

Boom!

The car exploded into a raging fireball. Aaron had rigged the detonation device to the gas cans in the trunk. Their microchips, and their former lives, were now gone.

They watched mesmerized for a few moments until they saw people running out of the store toward the burning car. Then they turned and disappeared into the night.

✍

Carol and Denise had been gone about thirty minutes when Aaron heard the sirens, and he hoped everything had gone as planned. He waited another twenty minutes before deciding he should drive over to Target in their remaining car. When he arrived, the smoldering remains of Carol's car was surrounded by three fire trucks still pouring water on it. He could only hope they had escaped.

He slept restlessly that night, half-expecting a call from the police, but he hadn't heard anything from them. Finally at 7 a.m. there was a knock at the door. Aaron slowly opened the door and saw two officers standing there.

"Mr. Shaw?" the taller officer asked.

"Yes, that's me," Aaron said. "I was just about to call you. My wife went shopping last night and hasn't returned. I hope you're bringing me some good news."

The officers glanced at each other, then the taller one said, "I'm Officer Peters and this is Officer Allred. We regret to inform you that your wife's car exploded last night in the Target parking lot."

"Exploded? Was she hurt? Was she still in the store?"

Officer Allred shook his head. "We ran a scan on her chip, and it was located inside the remains of the car after the firemen put the blaze out."

Aaron dropped to one knee and began to openly weep. This wasn't an act. He was truly relieved to hear that everything they'd planned had apparently fallen into place. The officers patted him on the back to comfort him.

Officer Allred then said, "I hate to add more bad news, but do you know someone named Denise Foster?"

"Yes, we've been taking care of her, because her parents disappeared in California. Is she all right?"

"Her chip was also found in the car. I'm sorry."

Aaron hung his head and let the tears flow for another couple of minutes before composing himself.

"What do I do now?" Aaron asked. "Can I identify the bodies?"

The policemen shook their heads again. "The fire was so hot that there really isn't anything left," Officer Peters said. "I'm sorry to say there aren't any identifiable remains left."

"What happened?" Aaron asked. "What makes a car explode for no reason?"

"We think it was intentionally set," Officer Peters said. "Did your wife have any enemies?"

"Well, we're Mormon, but other than that, I didn't think so. This is so terrible!" Aaron bent over slightly, truly feeling nauseated from the stress of the past few hours. "I'm sorry, but I feel so weak. I need to rest."

The officers helped him to the couch and Officer Allred brought him a glass of water from the kitchen.

"We'll check back with you later today and let you know if we find anything else," Officer Allred said. "Once again, we're sorry to have to bring you this news."

They shut the door, and Aaron lay quietly. He was happy their plan had worked, but he was also grieving. Without Carol, he now felt completely alone.

"My dear Carol, I'll find my way to you as soon as I can," he whispered.

CHAPTER 14

Nathan and Marie began their journey from Springfield to Nauvoo along the lonesome highways of rural Illinois. It felt like they were doing a succession of 5K races. They would walk for about 45 minutes, then they'd rest for a short time before starting again. Nathan had been pleased—and astonished—at Marie's rapid recovery from the Black Flu after the priesthood blessing. She seemed as strong as she'd ever been, and the dark splotches on her skin were fading rapidly.

As they traveled, they passed a succession of abandoned farmhouses. Even the small towns were empty. It looked like people had just given up and gone elsewhere even before the great storm destroyed the crops throughout the region.

"I'm surprised we haven't come across more people out here," Marie said.

"Me too, but I think I know the reason why," Nathan said, holding up the half-empty water bottle he'd been carrying. "I'll bet as the summer went on, the water supply got scarce, especially in the small towns where one family or group could probably take control of the water supply and deprive everyone else."

"That's true. Once someone cut off the water, I'll bet there was a mass exodus to the closest river or stream."

When they passed one particular farmhouse, the front door was wide open and most of the windows were broken. It was obvious no one was there, but Nathan was intrigued by several cars parked in a field near the house.

"Do you think any of those cars work?" he asked.

"It wouldn't hurt to check," Marie said. They approached the cars carefully, half expecting someone to jump out at them. As they got closer it was clear that this batch of cars hadn't moved in years.

"Look how the weeds have grown around the tires," Nathan said. "This isn't looking too promising."

"Oh well," Marie said. "Let's keep moving then."

They started walking back to the road, but Nathan felt drawn to a green Chevy Nova on the far end that looked like it was made in the 1970s. He peered in the window, and the gas gauge showed it had nearly a half tank of gas. He pulled on the door handle, and it opened. Instinctively, he lifted the floor mat and was shocked to see a set of keys.

"Yes! Marie, maybe we're in business!"

She stood nearby as he got behind the wheel and put the key in the ignition. When he turned it, the engine coughed twice.

Marie pounded on the hood. "Come on, you green monster! You can do it!"

The battery seemed to have a little bit of juice, and after three more tries, the engine roared to life. Marie opened the passenger door, tossed their remaining food and the wheelchair in the back seat, then hopped in. Nathan put the gas pedal to the floor, and they bounced across the field at twenty miles per hour, but it felt like they were rocketing along.

"This is awesome!" Marie said as they pulled onto the pavement. Nathan started down the road toward Nauvoo, but he suddenly parked the car and jumped out.

"What's wrong?" Marie asked.

"I was worried the tires would be flat. They're a little low, but it looks like they'll hold up."

"I'm glad," Marie said, "but I would've told you to drive on the tire rims, to be honest."

When they got rolling again, Marie stuck her head out the window, enjoying the breeze. Nathan kept an eye on the gas gauge, and it was dropping fairly steadily. "It looks like we've got a gas guzzler, but we'll enjoy it while it lasts," he said.

Marie turned on the car radio and slowly moved the dial through the whole spectrum, but all she found was static.

"I would've thought we'd find something out there," she said. "I would've even been happy to find a rap music station."

"I think things are worse off throughout the country than we can imagine," Nathan replied. "I'm sure Chicago is in complete chaos now. Hopefully we can get an update on things when we reach the temple."

Their joyride lasted for just over an hour, but they were able to cover fifty miles before the car sputtered and rolled to a stop on the outskirts of Carthage, Illinois. They pulled the wheelchair out of the backseat and stacked the food in it before bidding farewell to the Chevy Nova.

"I wish the ride had lasted longer, but that sure was a lot of fun," Marie said. "It's amazing all of the conveniences we used to take for granted."

꩜

As they walked into the town, Nathan glanced at Marie, wondering if she would notice the small billboard on the right side of the road. Suddenly she pointed it out.

"Hey look! The Carthage Jail! Isn't that where Joseph Smith and his brother Hyrum were killed?"

"It is," Nathan said, suddenly feeling a surge of emotion. "We certainly ought to see it. The sign says it's on Buchanan Street."

Like the other small towns they had passed through since leaving Springfield, they didn't see anyone.

It didn't take long for them to find Buchanan Street, and within a few minutes they were standing in front of the two-story brick building where the two prophets were shot to death in 1844.

"Do you feel anything?" Nathan said, on the verge of tears.

Marie nodded. "Actually yes. I know we're walking on sacred ground. Let's go inside."

They climbed the stairs to the second-floor room where the confrontation took place. The Spirit was strong as Nathan told Marie how an angry mob had burst through the door and shot Hyrum in the face. Joseph had turned to leap out of the window, but bullets struck him from both sides. He fell from the window and died on the ground below.

"It's terrible what people will do to each other," Marie said softly as she envisioned the scene.

They stepped outside and walked to a statue of Joseph and Hyrum standing together that they had noticed from the window. The two brothers looked strong and fearless, yet calm.

Nathan reached out and touched Joseph's arm. "The mob that killed them all those years ago thought they'd killed the Church too," he said. "But Joseph himself taught that the Church would roll forth and fill the whole earth in preparation for the Second Coming. It's an honor to be a part of it."

❧

After leaving Carthage, they traveled a few more miles and then slept in a barn for the night. The next morning they reached Nauvoo and could see the temple's tower in the distance, with the Angel Moroni on top.

"I'm so glad the temple hasn't been damaged," Marie said.

When they were within a couple of blocks of the temple, a man holding a rifle stepped out into the road. Nathan and Marie stopped in their tracks as the man motioned toward the wheelchair.

"What's under that blanket?" he asked, keeping his finger on the trigger.

"Just some food," Nathan said. "We've been traveling from Chicago. We're Latter-day Saints."

The man relaxed a little. "As you've noticed, we're a little off the beaten path. We haven't had many people come through town lately. How is it out there?"

"Not good. There's a lot of violence, and the Black Flu seems to be coming back for another round."

"I don't like the sound of that," the man said, still somewhat on the defensive. "So how can I help you?"

"We're hoping to reach the temple grounds to rest a little, then we'll help out however we can."

The man shook his head. "I'm sorry, but no one is allowed onto the temple block right now. You're welcome to go to one of the Church camps, though. There's one a few miles away across the river. I can give you directions."

Nathan smiled. "I know you're just doing your assignment, but I'm a maintenance missionary, and I have the password."

The man's demeanor changed completely. "Why didn't you just say that? So I suppose you don't have the chip."

"We're both clean," Marie said.

The man nodded. "Go to the front gate and give the password to one of the guards."

They thanked him for letting them through and then began walking again toward the temple.

"It sounds like they're encouraging people to settle elsewhere," Marie said. "I guess I expected Nauvoo to be a bustling little Mormon village."

Nathan shrugged. "There's probably a small group of guards watching over the Church's property—like the man we just talked to. The righteous Saints are gathered in the safest camps, and the stragglers are in other camps where at least there is a decent supply of food and water. I'm sure that's where he was trying to send us."

As they approached the main gate to the temple grounds a few minutes later, they saw a middle-aged man crouched down, checking on some flowers along a walkway.

"Hello," Nathan called out.

The man stood up in surprise, and then waved. "Welcome to Nauvoo. The temple grounds are closed, though. Sorry."

He quickly began walking away. Nathan and Marie glanced at each other, and she said, "These guys sure are good at sending people on their way."

"D&C 4:7," Nathan called out, and the man stopped in his tracks, then turned to them with a twinkle in his eye.

"Anything else you'd like to add?" he asked as he stepped toward the gate.

"Ask, and ye shall receive; knock, and it shall be opened unto you. Amen."

"That is correct," the man said, acknowledging the Church's password. "I assume you can vouch for this lovely young lady?"

"Yes. I'm Nathan and this is Marie. We've come from Chicago, and we don't have the chip. I'm a maintenance missionary, and we're here to help you if you need us."

"It's a pleasure to meet you," the man said as he opened the gate. "I'm Daniel Golding, the temple president. We can certainly use your help. We're down to a skeleton crew of senior missionaries here, plus a few men stationed at each of the main entry points who guard the city. Did you encounter one of them on your way here?"

"Yes, we met a guard—and his rifle," Marie said as she pushed the wheelchair through the gate and lifted the blanket. "This is our food supply. You're welcome to have it."

"Thank you," President Golding said, looking at their dwindling pile of canned food. "We're well-stocked, though, with a variety of meals."

Marie sighed. "Good. I'm dying to have a warm dinner."

"We can arrange that," the president said. He led them onto the temple grounds, where they met a few others and shared their story of traveling from Chicago. The group mainly consisted of older couples. One of the men put his hand on Nathan's shoulder and said, "We're sure grateful the Lord has sent some young blood our way."

They chuckled, and President Golding said, "It's interesting how the Lord has led us all to this place. For example, just before things got really bad across the nation, I felt compelled to move here and work as a manager at Hotel Nauvoo. At first it seemed like I'd made a big mistake, but then I was called to be the temple president when the previous one passed away suddenly. Now I know this is where I'm supposed to be."

"I know what you mean," Marie said, glancing at Nathan. "The Lord is watching over us."

She had come to realize that the Chicago internship wasn't what the Lord had intended for her, but through it all she had grown spiritually and become a better person in ways she likely wouldn't have if she'd stayed in Utah.

"Speaking of the hotel, that's where we've been staying," President Golding said. "With the guards in control of the main roads, we feel safe sleeping there. And since it looks like you'll be joining us, let's get a room for you two as well."

Nathan raised his hand. "Uh, I just want to clarify that we aren't married—and we haven't been acting like it either."

President Golding raised his eyebrows. "I just assumed . . ."

Marie laughed. "That's understandable, but we'll take separate rooms."

"Separate rooms it is!"

❧

A few hours later, Marie knelt by her bed in the hotel. They had been treated wonderfully by the temple workers, who had fed them a delicious meal and let them take their first showers in months. The water had been cold, but delightful all the same.

She had said good-night to Nathan a few moments earlier, and it was going to feel strange not having him within an arm's length. She said a quick prayer, and then climbed into the bed. The clean sheets felt like heaven.

"My own bed!" she chortled. They didn't have electricity or warm water, but she felt happier than she had in years.

Marie was surprised as a burning filled her chest and then spread throughout her body, as if the Holy Ghost was letting her know she was on the right track. It was a feeling that had been absent for a long time until Nathan had returned to her life.

"Thank thee, dear Lord, for Nathan," she whispered. "Please help me to never again leave the straight and narrow way."

CHAPTER 15

That same evening, Garrett sat in the front passenger seat of a U.N. transporter, pointing his chip detector toward an apartment building in southern Los Angeles. The device gave several beeps, and the driver stopped the vehicle near the front door.

Garrett climbed out and held up seven fingers to several peacekeepers who were standing in the back of the vehicle. They quietly stepped out onto the street, then some of them went in the front door, while the rest ran around the building to secure any other entrances.

"If they catch all seven of them, that will probably be enough for today," Garrett told the driver, the only other person among his group who spoke English. "That would give us about twenty captives in the back cage right now."

Garrett stood on the sidewalk and waited for the soldiers to bring their newest captives out of the building. A movement caught his eye, and he saw a waif-like Latino girl peek her head out of a nearby alley. He could have sworn it was his daughter Denise, but maybe his eyes were playing tricks on him. He hurried into the alley and saw the girl cowering behind a tipped-over garbage can.

"I won't hurt you," he told her.

As he reached her, he saw she was holding a tiny baby wrapped in a dirty blanket. It wasn't his daughter, but the girl could've been Denise's twin.

"Everything is okay," he told her. "Is this your baby?"

The girl nodded meekly. "I gave birth a couple days ago. I'm afraid he's not going to live."

"You gave birth alone?" Garrett asked, and she nodded again.

"Come with me," he said. "I can save your son."

She stood up and Garrett put his arm around her shoulders as they walked back to the transporter. He opened the passenger door and motioned for her to sit in the front seat.

The driver angrily said, "She can't be up here! She belongs in the back with the others!"

Garrett stared silently at him, causing the driver to look away as the girl took a seat between them.

"Go straight to the hospital," Garrett said. "We can come back for the others. This girl and her baby need immediate help."

"Sir, this isn't protocol," the driver muttered. "We don't have time for this. If they die, they die."

Garrett glared at him. "You know what? We've got all the time in the world. These captives aren't going anywhere. Drive to the hospital. It's only a few blocks."

The girl looked up at Garrett and mouthed, "Thank you."

The U.N. had reopened five hospitals to care for people who could potentially help rebuild the city. Garrett knew that his driver didn't feel the girl deserved to be saved, but the driver also knew he had pushed Garrett's buttons too much already. He didn't want to be reassigned to a worse task, such as unloading the latest cargo shipments down at the port.

During their drive to the hospital, Garrett quietly checked the girl's chip information and learned that her name was Sonia Mendoza. She was apparently fifteen years old but looked younger. When they arrived, he helped her from the vehicle and led her to a nurse, who snapped to attention when she saw Garrett approach in his U.N. uniform.

"Please make this young girl and her baby your top priority," he told her. "She's important to me."

The nurse nodded and began to lead Sonia to an examination room, but the girl looked back at Garrett and asked, "Sir, what is your name?"

"Garrett Foster."

She wiped away a tear. "Then my baby is going to be named Garrett Foster Mendoza. I'll never forget you, and when he gets older, I'll tell him you saved his life."

Garrett felt a rush of emotion as he waved good-bye to her. Here—among all the destruction—was a glimmer of hope.

"I'm honored," he said with emotion. "May God bless you."

Following the trip to the hospital, they returned to the previous building, where the forces were waiting with the seven captives that Garrett had located with his chip detector. They squeezed them into the cage in the back of the transporter and dropped them off at the collection area. Garret could finally call it a day.

It was the culmination of a very long week for him. Just seven days earlier, the streets of Los Angeles had been empty and it appeared that very few people were still living in the city. However, according to reports from the government's NSA database of chip implants, there were still thousands of people alive there.

So the first assignment for the U.N. troops was to get those people to come out of hiding. Garrett felt it wasn't worth the effort, but the U.N. officials told him it would be difficult to rebuild the city without knowing who actually still lived there. Garrett knew the real reason—the U.N. wanted to eliminate any chance someone might organize an underground group that would rise up and oppose them.

Since the city and state governments had essentially evaporated in the months since the earthquake, the U.N. leaders had decided to make the Los Angeles City Hall their headquarters. This choice was mainly for symbolic reasons, although the building had held up well in the earthquake and the U.N. technicians had figured out how to get several generators working to provide electricity to the building. This allowed them to operate their computers and maintain contact with the Coalition leaders overseas.

Garrett was hearing enough about the Coalition from other

leaders to realize that this peacekeeping effort had darker purposes. He had attended a key meeting at City Hall earlier in the week, where the leaders offered several fairly violent plans on how to herd the people to a central location, but Garrett shook his head at each suggestion. The ideas might have worked in China where the people more willingly obeyed, but Americans needed to be offered some incentives. In these dire times, most citizens still wondered, "What's in it for me?"

Garrett stood in the back of the room with other soldiers as the leaders argued, but finally he walked to the front and said, "You're making this too complicated. You need to lure them out with sweetness and honey, not through intimidation."

Garrett suggested the U.N. peacekeepers outfit several vehicles with loudspeakers and drive along the streets of the city broadcasting a message of peace in several languages. He added, "After all, we're supposed to be peacekeepers, aren't we?"

The U.N. officials looked at each other and smiled. "You're right," the top official told him. "And since you're an American, why don't you be the voice?"

Garrett was happy to oblige, and he even helped write the message. By that afternoon he had recorded: *"Dear citizens, I am Corporal Garrett Foster of the United States Army. Please don't fear the peacekeepers from the United Nations. They are here to protect us and provide us with food and medical care. Gather to the closest post office or public library to receive the help you need. Don't be afraid. They only want to help us. All is well, and we will rebuild this city better than before."*

For the next couple of days Garrett's message repeatedly echoed throughout the streets of Los Angeles, along with versions in other languages recorded by other soldiers. Garrett got tired of hearing his own voice, but the plan worked better than expected. By sunset the streets were filled with people, and long lines had formed outside the public buildings. The people came in all shapes and sizes, but mostly they were hungry, unbathed, and frazzled.

When there were disturbances in the lines, thankfully there

were plenty of U.N. soldiers with guns to keep the unruly ones from getting out of control. By midnight almost everyone who had emerged from hiding had a full stomach and were registered in the U.N.'s database. They were told to stay nearby, because breakfast would be served starting at 7 a.m.

However, they weren't told that after breakfast they would be forcibly marched to major outdoor venues such as the Rose Bowl, the Los Angeles Coliseum and Dodger Stadium for additional "evaluations" by the U.N. peacekeepers.

᠁

After the success of Garrett's plan, he had been quickly promoted through the ranks. The top U.N. leaders liked him, and he was now allowed the privilege of having his own sleeping quarters in City Hall. His superiors were pleased with how he was serving as the lead commander on one of the transporters, because the peacekeepers had come from many nations, and most of them didn't speak English. He'd been able to diffuse several tense situations by simply understanding the American way of thinking. He pleaded for peace several times when citizens had wanted to fight the U.N. forces, sparing both sides a lot of needless bloodshed through his actions.

While living in City Hall, Garrett learned that similar contingents of U.N. peacekeepers were now on the East Coast and in cities along the Gulf of Mexico, with plans to move inland soon. The official "company line" from the U.N. leaders was that they were simply doing this out of the goodness of their hearts to provide relief and aid to American citizens, but as the days went on, Garrett saw more indications that the freedoms the Americans had given up under martial law weren't going to be restored anytime soon.

Unfortunately, the U.S. government—at least what was left of it—apparently supported the U.N.'s efforts, so there wasn't much to argue about, despite how much he loved his country. He had only joined up with the U.N. because he'd had no other choice. At least he was still alive to possibly do something about America's situation later on. Sometimes when he went to bed, his conscience bothered him for promoting the U.N.'s agenda, but he figured that by acting as a mediator he was helping his fellow Americans avoid painful, unnecessary deaths.

He couldn't deny, though, that he truly despised what many Americans had become. Even after several months on a limited diet in primitive conditions, many of these people still had big bellies, flabby chins and a general unhealthy appearance. They also had foul mouths and an unwarranted "holier than thou" attitude toward the peacekeepers. There were times when Garrett wanted to slap them and say, "Wake up and behave yourselves so they'll keep treating you nicely! We blew it! The good times are gone!"

⬿

Garrett yearned to know the true fate of Vanessa and Denise, but so far he hadn't been able to find out where they were. The chip detector he used each day was a basic model that didn't allow him to access information on people outside the area.

Then one evening at City Hall, he saw a U.N. official using a computer to check the chip status of citizens who had been captured. Garrett watched him from a distance for a minute, then finally walked toward him.

"Hello, can I ask you a favor?" Garrett asked.

He'd never met the man before, but the man recognized Garrett's voice from the message they'd all heard repeatedly.

"Ah! You the . . . voice!"

Yes," Garrett said with a smile. "I want to find my wife. I think she is dead. Can you check?"

The man nodded, and Garrett gave him Vanessa's information. The computer searched for a few seconds, then the word "Asleep" appeared next to her picture.

"Very pretty," the man said. "I'm sorry."

"Me too."

Garrett read the details, and he wasn't surprised to discover she had died at Huntington Memorial Hospital in Pasadena. As he had suspected, her body had likely been one of those he'd seen in the hospital parking lot. It broke his heart, but it was a relief to know for certain that she wasn't suffering somewhere.

"One more," he said softly to the soldier. "My daughter."

They soon called up Denise's information, and Garrett was shocked to see the reading, "Asleep/Fugitive" as her chip status. He read the description of how her chip was recovered from a burned-out car that had been owned by Aaron and Carol Shaw.

Garrett shook his head in frustration. The official status was that Denise had died in the car fire, but there were many questions surrounding the incident, and her status wasn't officially determined. Carol had also apparently died in the fire, but her chip status matched Denise's, meaning there were unanswered questions about her death as well.

He shook his head and whispered, "I need to somehow get to Utah."

CHAPTER 16

Aaron Shaw lay awake at 5 a.m., staring blankly into the darkness of his bedroom. He hadn't slept well since Carol and Denise had departed for the mountain camp a few days earlier. He realized how much Carol had been an anchor for him during his stressful service as a "double agent" for the Church. He wished he could just hear her voice to know she was making good progress to the Kamas campground where their ward members were.

When the bedroom alarm clock sounded at 6 a.m., he turned it off and then wandered to the kitchen, where he knelt down at a chair to pray before consuming a bowl of cold cereal and two pieces of toast. He admitted that his soul was weary not only because Carol was gone, but because his job was so depressing. The last couple days had been devoted to tallying up the dead in major cities along the East Coast.

This data was being passed along to the U.N. peacekeepers, who were making inroads in California, New York, New Jersey, Pennsylvania, Florida, and Texas. They were working their way inland, and it gave Aaron a bad feeling. The U.S. president had addressed the nation again, thanking the citizens for their cooperation in allowing the peacekeepers to help America get back on its feet, but his words were hollow, as if a larger power was telling him what to say.

It also bothered Aaron that the president had never given a departure date for these U.N. forces, and he sensed they might never leave. It felt like the Mountain West was an island of normalcy, while the rest of the nation was on the verge of embracing either anarchy or tyranny. He wasn't sure which one would be worse.

Orem had been able to keep its power grid functioning most of the time, and Aaron was grateful for that, but he wondered how long basic food items would be available to the public, since the nation's commercial trucking industry was basically at a standstill after the big storm. He and Carol had stored a lot of food in the basement, and he'd survive on his own for several weeks, but he felt it wouldn't be long before his neighbors came knocking on his door for handouts.

≈

Aaron was soon driving north on Redwood Road through Saratoga Springs. Traffic was sparse, and some mornings it seemed like the only people on the road were his fellow government employees heading to the NSA Utah Data Center or to nearby Camp Williams. Most everyone else was out of work and had no reason to be on the road at that early hour. One perk of working for the federal government was the gasoline allowance that was automatically deposited into his account each month. It helped cover his travel expenses after the price of gas had started to soar that summer. He wasn't sure how private businesses even stayed afloat with the economy tanking—although there weren't too many small businesses still around anyway.

Soon the data center was visible ahead. Aaron noticed there was a long line of cars backed up to make the lefthand turn into the center's parking lot, so he slowed down to about 20 miles per hour.

Suddenly the car lurched forward, as if it had been bumped from behind. Aaron angrily checked his rearview mirror, but the closest car was a red Nissan about 30 feet behind him.

"Have I blown a tire?" he thought, slowing to a crawl as he pulled to the side of the road. Then he heard a very loud rumbling, as if he were standing next to the tracks while a freight train approached. Suddenly the car somehow jerked upward, and only Aaron's seatbelt keep him from hitting his head on the roof of the car. He looked around and saw other vehicles doing the same bouncy maneuver. It finally dawned on him this was a severe earthquake—and possibly the Big One that the citizens of Utah had been anticipating for decades.

The red Nissan that had been trailing him now swerved past. The driver was a co-worker named Whitney Vincent, and she was screaming in terror as her car skidded toward a five-foot-wide crack that had opened in the pavement. She tried to turn, but instead her car jolted to a stop with a sickening crunch as the front end dipped into the crevasse.

Everything seemed to be in commotion as Aaron leaped out of his car to help her. He only made it two steps before stumbling to his knees. The ground beneath him was gyrating like a big bowl of Jell-O. The intense shaking continued for at least two more minutes, although it seemed much longer. Aaron could only crouch down and pray for the earthquake to stop.

When the ground finally started to settle, Aaron hurried over to Whitney's car. She was lying motionless inside, and her neck was twisted at a strange angle. He tried to open the door, but the bottom of the car's frame had actually bent and the door wouldn't budge.

He grabbed a chunk of broken pavement and smashed in the car's passenger window. After clearing away the pieces of glass, he reached in to assist Whitney. He checked for a pulse, but there wasn't one. He could now see that her legs had been crushed in the impact, and blood filled the bottom of the car. She appeared to have been killed instantly.

Aaron turned away in shock, realizing it might have been him in that crevasse if he hadn't pulled over to the side of the road.

"I'm so sorry, Whitney," Aaron said, gently reaching over and closing her eyes as the ground began to rock again. Landslides had started cascading down the nearby hills.

As the latest rumbling subsided, Aaron started walking north on Redwood Road toward the data center. He prayed in his heart that Carol and Denise were safe somewhere in the mountains, then he focused on his own troubles. The road was broken up in several places, so he had to be careful as he walked, but after about ten minutes he reached the gate to the parking lot.

From what he could see, several of the center's buildings were damaged, with cracks in the walls or broken windows. There was a plume of smoke coming from a building on the north side, but he couldn't see any flames.

Several of his co-workers had also abandoned their cars and were gathered outside the entrance gate, where five guards were blocking the roadway. Aaron saw a co-worker named Tom Granger near the front of the group, so he went to his side.

"What's going on?" Aaron asked him.

"They won't let us in," Tom said. "They claim they're in lockdown mode because they think the data is somehow vulnerable in all of this confusion. But we all know this place has a series of back-up battery sites. The power never goes out here."

"Besides, it's not like someone could come in and carry it away," Aaron said. "It's all digital."

"You're right, but some bigwig has made the decision, so even though these guards have scanned our chips each morning for months and know our faces, they aren't budging."

"That's strange," Aaron said. "It's not like any of us want to work today. We just want to patch up our injuries and maybe help put out that fire."

Tom nodded. "Exactly."

"You knew Whitney Vincent pretty well, didn't you?" Aaron asked. "I've got some bad news. I saw her crash her car during the quake, but she was dead by the time I could reach her."

"That's awful," Tom said, visibly shaken. "I can't believe it. Where is she?"

"Still in her car about a quarter-mile down the road. I couldn't get her out."

Aaron's comment about Whitney seemed to trigger something dark in Tom. Suddenly he moved toward one of the guards and shouted, "Come on, let us in! People are injured and dying out here. You know we're not a threat."

"Don't come any closer," the guard said anxiously, backing up a couple of steps and pointing his pistol at Tom's chest. "I have orders to shoot to kill."

"You'd really shoot me for trying to help a co-worker?" Tom asked. "My friend Whitney is dead, and I'm going to call her family. Step aside and let me in."

The guard shook his head. "That's my orders. Now move back with the others."

For some reason, Tom wouldn't drop the subject. He argued long enough that three of the five guards were soon screaming obscenities in his face.

"*Get out of here,*" the Spirit whispered to Aaron, and he quickly backed away down the road as most of the crowd surged forward to support Tom. Within seconds, Aaron heard several shots fired, and all he could see was a flailing mass of humanity as the guards were overpowered and beaten by the workers.

Aaron turned and ran north on Redwood Road toward Salt Lake without looking back. There were others walking from that direction toward the data center, and when they'd ask him to stop and explain what happened, he'd just say, "Don't go that way. It's bad. They're killing each other."

After running for about a mile, he noticed that the destruction seemed to be getting worse. He looked toward the Point of the Mountain, but it didn't look the same. A big chunk of it seemed to be missing.

He finally slumped down behind the shade of an abandoned car and let his emotions pour out. He started sobbing and couldn't stop. Utah had been spared much of the nation's recent catastrophes, but he knew nothing would ever be the same again.

He was sickened by the actions of his co-workers. Only an hour earlier, they had been upstanding citizens on their way to work. Now after the earthquake, they had already exhibited signs of savagery and a mob mentality. He was sure Tom and several others had been shot to death, and the guards probably hadn't survived either.

On impulse he picked up a rock, then stood up and smashed it through the car's passenger window. It was the second window he'd shattered in the past hour. The first time had been in an effort to save Whitney, and now he was doing it to save his own life. He carefully searched through the pieces of glass on the passenger seat until he found one the right size.

"Mr. President, please accept my resignation," he said solemnly as he sliced open the back of his hand. He then used the glass to dig out his chip. He let his hand bleed as he held the chip and looked closely at it.

"Oh, what fools we've been," he said. "Our freedoms are gone, and we're being led like sheep to the slaughter."

He let the chip fall to the pavement, then he kicked it into the weeds alongside the road.

"Good riddance," he said as he put pressure on his bleeding hand. He started walking along Redwood Road again toward Salt Lake. He was feeling calm and ready for the next phase of his life. The Church was his only employer now.

Chapter 17

Several minutes earlier, Carol and Denise had stood along the eastern railing of the Deer Creek Reservoir dam. They looked across the shimmering water.

"We just need to stay on this road for a few more miles, then we'll reach Heber," Carol said, pointing across the reservoir at a distant community. "Then we'll almost be getting close to the camp where our friends and neighbors are."

"Okay," Denise said with a slight smile. "The hike can't be much worse than the one we just finished."

"That's for sure," Carol answered. "My legs are screaming for a break, but let's keep going for a little while."

Their journey up Provo Canyon had been more strenuous for Carol than she'd ever imagined when she and Aaron had devised their plan. Part of the problem was that there had been more people and vehicles traveling in the canyon than they thought there would be, so Carol and Denise had stayed off the highway and the paved canyon trail as much as possible to stay out of sight and avoid encountering other people.

Also, Carol was out of shape and had quickly developed blisters, which had slowed their pace considerably. Thankfully Denise had been patient with her, and she now felt renewed energy as she looked across the reservoir.

They finished walking across the dam and then had no choice but to stay on the highway, since they had towering cliffs on the south side of the road and the reservoir on the other. Thankfully no vehicles could be seen in either direction as they hurried along that stretch before the valley opened up a little and the road began to climb above the shoreline. Carol paused to bask in the sunshine when a queasy sensation passed through her.

Whoom, whoom.

Carol turned to Denise. "Did you hear that?"

Suddenly the pavement beneath them jolted sideways, violently knocking them both down. The ground rumbled and groaned beneath them for nearly a minute as they stayed on their backs and held their heads with their hands, trying to avoid getting too banged up by the asphalt.

The initial jolt soon subsided, but as they sat up and looked around, they gasped as they saw the reservoir. It had been calm just two minutes earlier, but now it was filled with large waves racing in all directions and crashing against the shoreline.

"Look at that!" Denise cried as a large landslide gained momentum down a nearby mountain and slammed into the water, causing even more disruption.

Crack!

They both instinctively ducked as the cliff they had just walked beneath collapsed and buried the highway less than 100 yards behind them. Dust filled the air from other smaller landslides, and the water in the reservoir continued to slosh violently.

As another tremor struck, Carol took Denise by the arm and led her to an open area south of the highway where they were in less danger of getting injured as the earth continued to shake.

"Are you all right?" Denise asked, pointing at Carol's bloodied arms and hands she'd suffered during the initial jolt.

"I've got a few gashes, but I'll survive," Carol said. "How about you?"

"I'm okay, but I cracked my knee pretty hard on the ground. It really hurts."

Denise then looked past Carol toward the northeast, and her eyes grew wide. "What's that?"

Carol turned toward Heber, and it took her a moment to comprehend what she was seeing. A blue-green wall of water was roaring out of the canyon north of the city.

"Holy smokes!" Carol cried. She grabbed Denise's hand and started running up a nearby hillside. She glanced back every few seconds, and each time she did, the water had grown closer and seemingly deeper. Heber had been completely engulfed. There were cars, yard items, and even parts of houses being tossed around at the front of the churning deluge.

"I don't get it. Where's the water coming from?" Denise asked as they paused to catch their breath.

"The Jordanelle Reservoir dam must've burst," Carol said. "This is really bad. Keep going!"

They climbed another 50 feet up the hillside before turning to watch the wave bury the town of Charleston and merge with the reservoir. The churning water zipped across the surface, combining to create a monster wave that barrelled toward the dam. The water quickly rose above the height of the Heber Creeper railroad tracks on the northern shore and wiped out the buildings near the boat harbors.

"It's never going to hold," Carol said, putting her hand to her forehead as she focused her eyes on the dam.

A thirty-foot wall of water slammed into the dam, and they could feel the impact from where they stood. The water seemed to recoil for an instant before rushing into the narrow canyon below, forming a bottleneck that completely engulfed the dam and caused the water to climb the canyon walls.

"Oh no," Denise cried. "It's going to reach us!"

Carol didn't respond. She was still intensely watching the area now covered with water where the dam had been. If it stayed intact, maybe that initial surge would be the extent of the damage downstream. Her heart dropped, though, as the entire mass of water seemed to start shifting toward the canyon.

"The dam is gone," Carol said quietly, thinking of the people near the mouth of Provo Canyon. They weren't going to have a chance to escape.

She closed her eyes and shuddered. They'd crossed the dam less than an hour earlier. She'd felt compelled to keep walking rather than rest that morning as they had hiked, and those extra few minutes were now the difference between life and death for them.

"We need to pray," she said, putting her arm around Denise. "I'll say it."

Denise nodded and closed her tear-filled eyes.

"Dear Heavenly Father, thank thee for sparing our lives this morning," Carol said. "We ask for thy protection and guidance at this time, and please prompt those downstream in Provo and Orem to take whatever action they need to. Please watch over my dear husband Aaron at this time . . ."

Carol felt such a strong surge of emotion that she couldn't speak. If she lost Aaron, she wasn't sure she could handle it, but after nearly a minute of silence she added, ". . . but thy will be done, Father."

CHAPTER 18

At that moment, Aaron was standing on a hillside above Camp Williams, near the line dividing Utah and Salt Lake counties. He had left Redwood Road a few minutes earlier and moved higher to get a better view of the damage the earthquake had caused.

He looked east again across the valley toward the Point of the Mountain and could better see how the intensity of the quake had shaken the sandy hill so badly that it had shifted in both directions, lowering it at least 100 feet. Unfortunately, the homes built on Traverse Mountain had all received major damage. Some had split in half as their foundations shifted, while others actually slid down the hill and had stopped at crazy angles.

Below those homes, the Cabela's store had sunk into the ground until only its green roof was visible, while the Adobe building had cracked in half where the main road passed beneath it.

"That fancy glass architecture didn't work out so well," Aaron muttered.

He started walking north again along the hillside, feeling an urgent desire to reach Temple Square. He needed to talk to Elder Bushman to determine what to do next. He searched the valley floor ahead of him and spotted the Utah State Prison, but the area beyond that didn't look the same. The familiar buildings and trees were . . . gone.

Aaron gasped in shock as he realized that an area several miles wide had simply collapsed, creating a monstrous sinkhole that reached from Sandy on the east, across where I-15 had been, then west into Bluffdale. Inside the hole he could see the roofs of buildings that were at least ten stories high, so it was quite deep.

Aaron impulsively started running toward the hole, which was about two miles away but seemed much closer. He steered clear of the prison, where three buildings were in flames and he could hear cursing and screaming. It sounded like the prisoners were taking matters into their own hands.

He finally reached the edge of the hole, and he reeled back in shock at the enormity of the destruction. The sheer size of the hole boggled Aaron's mind. It was several miles wide. Thousands of homes and businesses had just sunk into the earth, including any citizens that happened to be there. The hole was partially filled with water that appeared to be rising.

He noticed a good chunk of I-15 was resting inside the hole. It reminded Aaron of the phrase in the Book of Mormon when cities were "swallowed up" at the time of the Savior's crucifixion.

A man riding a four-wheeler pulled up beside him. On the back of the vehicle was a set of ropes and harnesses.

"I don't know if there's anything we can do, but I ran home to get some of my rock-climbing equipment," the man said. "Do you want to help me?"

"Sure," Aaron said. "Are there survivors?"

"I'm afraid most of the people were either crushed or drowned, but I heard some calls for help earlier. I'm Dale, by the way."

"Nice to meet you. I'm Aaron. This is so unbelievable. What do you think happened?"

"It must've been an underground lake," Dale said. "It looks like the roof of the cavern simply collapsed."

They walked along the edge of the crater, looking for any signs of life, but it was eerily quiet. Most of the houses were completely submerged or only had their roofs showing. As they walked along, more bodies became visible in the water.

"I don't think there's anything we can do here," Dale said sadly. "What a tragedy."

A loud rushing sound could now be heard. They turned to see the Jordan River had suddenly turned into a torrent of water. It was overflowing its banks and seemed to be growing worse. The excess water found a path to the crater and began cascading into the hole.

"Where would that all be coming from?" Aaron asked.

"It's been almost two hours since the earthquake," Dale said. "If the reservoir dams up Provo Canyon broke, Utah Lake would rise quickly. I'll bet that's what has happened. Hop on back and we'll see."

Aaron climbed on the back of the four-wheeler, and as Dale steered them toward a ridge where they could see into Utah Valley, Aaron prayed that Carol and Denise had escaped the destruction.

Dale made his way to the 14600 South exit of I-15. They could see the prison again, and the water was now flooding the entire complex. There were men on top of the buildings looking for ways to escape.

Soon Dale stopped on a ridge overlooking Utah Valley and they dismounted. Aaron could hardly comprehend the sight below them. The lower valley areas all around Utah Lake were under water. Telephone and power poles, along with houses and cars, were jutting out of the water, and the gardens of Thanksgiving Point were now submerged. The Jordan River was now seemingly a half-mile wide as it tried to handle all of the massive flow.

"Whoa, that's a mess," Dale said, turning to look back at the Salt Lake Valley. "At least it looks like the temples are okay."

Aaron spotted the Draper Temple still intact a few miles to their right. The day before, the hill would have blocked the view, but the hill had slid enough that the temple could now be seen from where they stood. The Oquirrh Mountain Temple looked intact in the distance, but although he could see the Jordan River Temple spire, he sensed the temple's namesake was now flooding it.

"So are you LDS?" Aaron asked.

"I am," Dale said.

"So where is your family?"

Dale looked at the ground. "They're at the camps. I was too stubborn to go, but it's looking like the prophet might have been right after all. What about your family?"

"I really don't know," Aaron said, shaking his head. "It's a long story. I'm actually on an assignment for the Church, and I need to reach Temple Square to report to the General Authorities. I better start walking. "

"Nonsense," Dale said. "I'll give you a ride. I just filled the gas tank."

"I can't expect you to do that," Aaron said. "It's much too far for you to—"

"I'm helping you," Dale said with a burst of emotion. "I live on the other side of the Jordan River, and I'm pretty sure I'm not getting back home anytime soon. Besides, my sister Kathy lives near 4800 South and State Street. I really need to check on her, so let me at least take you that far."

Aaron nodded. "That would be great."

⚜

Dale carefully maneuvered their way north along the eastern foothills of the Salt Lake Valley. The earthquake's destructive power was clearly evident, but it was perplexing. One block of homes would be relatively unscathed, then the next one would look like a giant foot had stomped on all of the houses.

The streets were relatively quiet, which allowed them to travel rather quickly. There wasn't much debris blocking their path, so they just kept moving along at about 15 miles an hour.

Hundreds of people were outside their homes, but they hardly gave the four-wheeler a passing glance. For the most part the citizens seemed to be in shock and were mostly standing around talking among themselves.

"Reality hasn't set in yet for anyone," Aaron said to himself. "It's going to get a lot worse in the next couple of days."

After a two-hour journey, they arrived in Kathy's neighborhood. It had been hit pretty hard, and fallen trees blocked the roads. The homes had been jolted off their foundations, leaving nearly every house at an odd angle or partially collapsed.

"That's Kathy's house over there," Dale said.

They drove closer, and a middle-aged woman standing on the lawn spotted them. She threw her hands in the air and ran toward them in a panic.

"Oh, Dale, I hoped you'd come," she cried as they got off the four-wheeler. "Heidi is trapped in the basement! We can talk to her, but she says the water's getting higher."

Dale hurried over to the side of the house where several people were standing around anxiously. The house had collapsed on itself, and Aaron could see the face of a young girl peering up at them through what was once a window well.

"Uncle Dale! Help me!"

"Don't worry," Dale told her, reaching down and taking her hand through the small opening. "We'll get you out."

Aaron crouched beside him and could see Heidi huddled on top of a table with only a few inches of space between her head and the ceiling. The water was rising even as he watched.

Dale tried pulling on a piece of plywood near the opening, but as he did so, the whole house seemed to groan and lean even further toward them. They stepped back, half-expecting the house to collapse at any moment.

"That's not going to work, but we can't let her drown," Dale said softly to Aaron. "Are you willing to go down inside the house with me?"

Aaron put his hand on Dale's shoulder. "Let's go."

"We're going to go inside," Dale told Kathy. "Please stand here and keep Heidi calm."

The two men yanked open the front door, and the floor creaked as they stepped inside the living room. The earthquake had shifted two couches, a recliner and a coffee table together at the south end of the front room. Then a large entertainment center had toppled on top of everything else, blocking the hallway that led to the basement stairs.

"Let's pull things out of the way," Dale said. They spent a

precious two minutes standing the entertainment center back up so that they could climb into the hallway.

One of Kathy's other daughters came to the front door. "Mom said to hurry! The water is up to Heidi's neck!"

Dale rushed down the stairs and climbed into the water. There was barely enough clearance in the hallway for him to breathe, but they could hear Heidi's screams.

"Dale, this is crazy," Aaron said. "By the time you get back, this hallway's going to be filled. You'll never make it out."

Dale grimaced, knowing Aaron was right, but he said, "I'd never be able to live with myself if I didn't try. Pray for me."

Before Aaron could even react, Dale took a deep breath and plunged into the flooded hallway. Aaron stood in shock, knowing there would likely be two drownings in the next couple of minutes—Heidi, and then Dale in a vain rescue attempt. Could it really be their time to die?

As panic seized his heart, Aaron put both hands in the swirling water and said, "By the power of the Melchizedek Priesthood I hold, and in the name of Jesus Christ, I command this water to depart this basement!"

It sounded ludicrous even as he said it, but within two seconds of his command, the western wall of the basement cracked. Water began gushing into a six-inch wide gap, and the water level began to noticeably drop. Soon there was nearly a foot of clearance in the hallway.

"Dale, are you okay?" Aaron called out.

He didn't hear a reply, but he heard cheering outside of the house. He soon heard splashing, and he saw Heidi paddling her way toward him as the water continued to drain into the gap in the wall. Aaron took her hand and pulled her onto the stairs. Dale was right behind her, and they all instinctively embraced.

"Whew, that was too close for comfort," Dale said. Then he noticed the water flowing into the gap. "Did that just happen?"

Aaron nodded. "The wall cracked right after you dove into the water."

"It's a miracle," Dale said, shaking his head in amazement. "We wouldn't have survived without it."

Aaron smiled. "The Lord was definitely watching out for both of you."

Kathy appeared at the top of the stairs, and Heidi climbed upward to greet her mom. Dale and Aaron followed them back out of the house, and Aaron silently thanked Heavenly Father for honoring his priesthood request. It was one small incident in the midst of great tragedy, but it affirmed for Aaron that miracles had certainly not ceased. He knew that through this disaster the power of the priesthood would become more evident in the lives of the faithful Saints.

❧

An hour later, Aaron stood near a small campfire in Kathy's backyard roasting a hot dog. After the drama of the rescue, several families had come together to share whatever food they'd had in their refrigerators before it spoiled. The electricity was still out, and no one was expecting it to come back on anytime soon.

Aaron had decided to spend the night there. Even though the earthquake had only happened that morning, an element of lawlessness was already evident. Word had spread of shootings in a nearby cul-de-sac, and the men in the neighborhood were already planning how to defend their homes.

As evening approached, everyone stopped in their tracks as the sound of a helicopter could be heard. Aaron stepped out into the driveway for a better look, and he saw several military helicopters coming from the north. Some began circling over parts of the valley, including downtown Salt Lake. Another pair of helicopters spent a lot of time hovering over the sinkhole at the south end of the valley.

"They probably came from Hill Air Force Base," Dale said as he joined Aaron. "The government is checking things out."

"It's kind of surreal," Aaron said. "Here we are without power, and we haven't seen an emergency vehicle all day, yet they're burning all that fuel to take a look around."

Dale gave him a crooked smile. "You're not actually surprised, are you?"

"No, but hopefully we'll get some help soon."

CHAPTER 19

Garrett Foster walked through Los Angeles City Hall and headed toward his private room that same evening. He had spent a long day at the Rose Bowl evaluating the citizens who were detained there. Garrett felt empty inside after helping determine the fate of fellow U.S. citizens. Some would essentially become slaves to the U.N. to help rebuild society, while the rest who didn't measure up would be . . . well, he didn't like to think about their future.

The main corridor was strangely quiet, and he noticed people intently watching something on a TV screen in a large conference room. He stepped inside and saw video images of flooding and widespread devastation.

"Where is this?" he asked a U.N. worker from Europe who was standing nearby.

"Celt Lake Seetee," the man said. "A big earthquake."

Garrett felt like a sledgehammer had smacked him in the chest. The video switched to footage taken from a helicopter above the Utah State Capitol Building, and Garrett could clearly see flooding throughout the downtown area, including Temple Square.

Within the hour, there was a meeting called for top-level leaders in the main assembly room. A Russian leader known as Commander Klopov stood before them. He had treated Garrett with respect ever since the success of the voice message. He was also one of the few foreign leaders who spoke English quite well.

"As some of you know, there has been another large earthquake," Klopov said. "This one took place in the state of Utah, several hundred miles away from us in the Rocky Mountains. This is a prime opportunity for us to gain the sympathy of the people there, as well as put the U.N. infrastructure in place. We will leave a large contingent of soldiers here, but we need a strong core of leaders to make the journey. Has anyone here traveled to Utah before?"

Garrett raised his hand. "I've driven that freeway a dozen times. There are stretches where the earthquakes have probably broken up the roads, though."

"We'll use the large transporters," Klopov said. "They'll crawl right over most obstacles. Aren't Hoover Dam and Las Vegas between here and Utah? We've been asked to secure those areas as well."

"Yes," Garrett said. "We can do that on the way."

Klopov smiled. "It looks like we've found our battalion leader. Who would've thought an American would be so useful?"

The others in the room chuckled. Garrett smiled back, but he knew this group wouldn't hesitate to eliminate him if they no longer needed his services. It was worth the risk of failure, though, if it meant he could find a way to reunite once again with Denise and Nathan.

⌘

After the meeting, Klopov asked Garrett to join him to discuss additional details about Utah.

"We've really been impressed with you," Klopov told him as they waited for the room to empty. "Most of the American leaders haven't been cooperative, but you seem to have the same vision for this country as we do."

"I just want to help get this nation back on its feet and be productive again," Garrett said.

"Well put," Klopov said. "So do we."

They were now joined by two other high-ranking U.N. officials, and Klopov motioned toward a small room connected to the main assembly hall. "Let's go have a chat in there," he said.

Garrett felt a bit apprehensive to be alone with these three leaders, but he simply smiled and followed them into the room. There were four folding chairs arranged in a circle, as if this meeting wasn't just happenstance. The others sat down, so Garrett did as well. Their demeanor was still cheery, but Garrett felt chilled.

"We're pleased that you wish to help lead the expedition to the Rocky Mountains," Klopov said. "We need someone who knows the terrain and what to expect in each city along the way."

"Yes, I know that whole area," Garrett said, "and I even know some other routes if the main freeway is blocked."

"Excellent," Klopov said. "I'll be joining you, and I hope we can depart within a couple of days. There is one matter of business to finalize with you, though—your loyalty."

"What do you mean?" Garrett asked. "I've already told you I'm committed to rebuilding the nation."

Klopov smiled faintly. "Yes, but who are we rebuilding the nation for?"

Garrett was confused for a moment, then it all became clear. As he had already suspected, the acts of "humanitarian kindness" by the U.N. forces had deeper purposes.

"America is essentially dead," Klopov continued. "The United States will never return. Over the years your leaders unwittingly paved the way for a group of nations known as the Coalition to divide up America among themselves."

Garrett felt sick to his stomach. "That's not true. The American people will never allow it to happen. They'll fight back."

The other three men chuckled.

"The master plan is already underway," Klopov said. "So far we've met little resistance, which is good, because we don't want to destroy the infrastructure your people have so kindly built for us. But if anyone does fight back, we have invasion forces waiting to come ashore."

Garrett shook his head. How could he have been so blind? He stared into each man's eyes, and all he saw in them was darkness.

"What does that mean for me?" Garrett finally asked.

"It means you have a choice to make," Klopov said. "You can

fully commit to us, and all will be well. You have the potential to be one of our greatest leaders. After the occupation of America is complete, you'll be greatly rewarded for your contributions."

"And if I don't make that commitment?"

Klopov's eyes narrowed. "You will walk out of this room a faithful, devoted American who missed a golden opportunity."

The room went silent, but Garrett knew the rest of the story. If he was lucky, they'd kill him quickly. If not, he'd rot in a prison with the thousands of other Americans he'd helped round up the past few days.

Fleeting images of his children's faces flashed through his mind. He could die with honor, but then he'd never see Nathan and Denise again. If he supported the Coalition, though, he'd be on his way to Utah where he could hopefully reunite with them.

Garrett sat up straight in his chair and said, "I will join you."

"That's wonderful," Klopov said. "You've been a real strength for us. You won't regret this decision. Please stand up and raise your right hand to take the Coalition's oath of secrecy and commitment."

Garrett stood in front of Klopov and dutifully recited the Russian's words, trying to block out that he was pledging his life and talents to an organization he didn't believe in.

As Garrett finished repeating the oath, the other men clasped him on the shoulder and congratulated him. They all soon left the room, and as he walked back to his sleeping quarters, he felt a darkness creep into his soul. The Coalition's oath felt strangely familiar.

Then the truth hit him hard. The oath was basically a counterfeit version of promises he had made in the temples of the LDS Church. He had been excommunicated from the Church several years earlier for having an extramarital affair with Vanessa, but deep down he had still hoped to fulfill those promises someday. Had he just sold his soul?

That night Garrett lay on his bed curled up in a ball. His head pounded, and his chest felt heavy. As he pondered the direction his life had taken, he wanted to scream. For the first time, he wondered if it might have been better to die in the parking lot of that Pasadena hospital.

Chapter 20

On the same morning the earthquake struck Salt Lake, Nathan and Marie took a walk through Nauvoo, stopping to look at many of the historic sites. They held hands and rubbed shoulders, even though Nathan was a little worried they were breaking "missionary protocol."

They were now back on Nauvoo's Temple Square, and Nathan offered to help weed some flower beds with several other men. Marie saw it as an opportunity to talk privately with President Golding. She had noticed him standing across the street near the Joseph and Hyrum Smith Memorial, which depicted the brothers traveling on horseback.

She slowly approached him, because President Golding was now sitting on the memorial's base and seemed to be praying.

"I'm sorry to disturb you," Marie said when he raised his head. "I just had a question. We can talk later, though."

"You're fine," he said, straightening up. "Sometimes I find comfort over here near these two fine men. Anyway, maybe you and I are seeking an answer to the same question."

"I doubt it," Marie said.

"You might be surprised," President Golding said. "What did you want to ask?"

Marie smiled, suddenly unsure of herself. "Can maintenance missionaries ever get married?"

President Golding kept a straight face. "Why? Do you have someone in mind?"

Marie laughed. "You have a pretty good idea who it is."

"See, we really were pondering the same question," he said. "I saw you two walking together this morning, and a voice said to me, '*It is their time.*' I didn't get told what it was time for, but I think you've helped provide the answer."

"Is that why you were praying?" Marie asked.

"Yes. I don't want to interfere or be a meddling matchmaker, but the Spirit has confirmed to me that if you two choose to get married now, it would be all right. Don't you agree?"

Marie's heart skipped a beat. "I do. But don't you think it should be Nathan's idea?"

"Certainly," President Golding said. "Leave it up to me. Wait here."

ॐ

President Golding went back across the street and found Nathan still working in the flowerbeds.

"You're working too hard," the president said with a smile. "You need to leave something for the older men to do."

"I enjoy it," Nathan said. "If the world hadn't fallen apart, I might have become a landscaper."

The president motioned for him to join him under the shade of a tree. "That's an interesting statement. So if the world hadn't fallen apart, was there anyone you had your eye on?"

"You mean to marry?" Nathan asked, suddenly feeling a bit awkward. "I think it's obvious. I didn't risk my life in Chicago just because I thought Marie was a nice friend."

"Yes, I can tell you two are close."

Nathan shook his head. "Why are we even discussing this? I'm a maintenance missionary. It's not an option."

"Hmm."

Nathan stared at President Golding. "What does that mean? I could marry her now?"

"Well, this morning the Spirit told me, '*It is their time*' and I don't think it was about you two moving on to the Spirit World."

Nathan cocked his head and looked up at the temple, deep in thought. After a few moments, President Golding asked, "What's on your mind?"

Nathan turned back to him. "Well, Elder Miller discouraged us from having a girlfriend when we were setting up the camps and traveling a lot. Then he essentially sent us forth into the world and told us to follow the Spirit, which for me included finding Marie in Chicago and protecting her."

Nathan tried not to smile as he shared this with the president. Of course he wanted to marry Marie, but it just didn't seem possible until now.

"Before I became the temple president, I was a temple sealer and I'm still authorized to perform sealings," President Golding said. "If you both feel that you should be married, then we'll proceed. With everything going on in the world, who knows when you'll have the opportunity again? Maybe it isn't an accident you ended up in Nauvoo."

Nathan suddenly started fidgeting. "But what if she doesn't want to get married yet?"

The president put his hand on Nathan's shoulder. "All you can do is ask. I think I saw her across the street."

Nathan nodded and walked to where Marie still stood near the statues.

"Hey Marie, do you have a second I could talk to you?"

She gazed into his eyes. "I suppose."

Nathan got down on one knee. "I'm hoping this won't come as a surprise to you, but will you marry me?"

Even though she was expecting it, Marie's eyes teared up when Nathan actually said the words. She took his hand and pulled him to his feet.

"Of course," she said, giving him a big embrace. She glanced at the nearby statues. Joseph and Hyrum seemed to be smiling at each other in approval.

Nathan took Marie's hand as they walked back to the temple grounds where President Golding was waiting.

"What was the answer?" the president asked playfully.

Marie winked at him. "Believe it or not, I said yes."

"Congratulations," he said. "Have you set a wedding date?"

Marie laughed. "Boy, you sure are pushy, aren't you?"

"I feel we should get married today," Nathan said.

Marie's eyes grew wide. "Are you serious? We've only been engaged five minutes."

"It's not like we need to plan a wedding reception," Nathan said. "Why wait?"

Marie turned to President Golding. "What do you think?"

"It could be done," he said with a shrug. "The main obstacle is that you haven't received your endowment yet, but we've got a bunch of temple workers who would love to make it happen. Then I could perform the sealing afterward."

Marie bit her lower lip. "I wish my parents could be here, but I know they'll be happy whenever they find out. Let's do it."

🙶

They walked back over to the flowerbeds, where a dozen of the temple guards and their wives were still working.

"We have an announcement," President Golding said. "Today this wonderful couple is going to be sealed together for eternity."

"Hurray!" one woman said. "I'm thrilled for you."

"We all are," a man said. "That's great news! I'm still technically the county clerk, so I'll go down to the office and get the marriage license ready."

"Good thinking," President Golding said. "We want this to be official."

As the man departed, everyone started talking at once, but President Golding held up his hand. "Marie has never received her endowment, though. We'll need to take her through a session before the sealing. Are you willing to help us out?"

They all eagerly agreed, hopping up and heading toward the temple, leaving their gardening tools right there in the flower beds. Soon President Golding, Nathan and Marie were standing alone.

"I think they're excited for you," the president said.

Marie suddenly felt a little overwhelmed. "Where do I even start?"

Nathan put his arm around her. "Everything is going to be fine. The temple workers are going to treat you like royalty for the rest of the day."

President Golding nodded. "However, while they're getting the rooms ready, I'd like to make sure we do everything properly. Since I can't contact your bishop and stake president, I feel I should still go through the temple recommend questions with you, and explain some things you'll see and hear in the endowment. Is that all right?"

"Certainly," Marie said. A few minutes later she and President Golding were seated in his office. He went through the temple interview questions, and Marie breezed right through them, although she chuckled at the one about tithing.

"I'm a full tithe payer, because I haven't earned a dime in months," she said. "The funny thing is I never actually got paid for my internship. They covered my living and food expenses, and then they were going to pay me a lump sum once I was finished."

Marie paused and wiped her eyes. "I never sowed my wild oats or anything like that, but I've made some choices that weren't wise, although they seemed right at the time. I was too focused on finishing my education and starting a career."

"Did you ever consider serving a mission?" President Golding asked.

Marie nodded. "I used to tell everyone I'd be sending my mission papers in as soon as I could. But once I got to the University of Utah, I let that goal slip down my priority list. I kept telling myself I'd go on a mission after the next semester, then the one after that. Suddenly the years had rolled by. Then I got the Chicago internship, and that pushed any further mission plans aside."

President Golding sat back in his chair. "I appreciate your honesty, but I guess I'm a little surprised. From what I've seen, you're an absolute delight, and you literally radiate goodness. What caused this positive change of heart?"

Marie rolled her eyes. "I guess I can thank my internship for that as well. Within a few hours of arriving in Chicago, I knew I didn't fit in with the people at the company. I held strong to my values, though—other than getting the chip. But the real turning point for me was spending a week trapped in a museum on Navy Pier, not knowing whether a gang member was going to break through the door and kill me, or if I was going to starve to death. I prayed nearly every moment I was awake, and I got my priorities straightened out again. I pleaded with Heavenly Father to give me one more chance, and He did. It's an absolute miracle that Nathan found me. I emerged from that museum a changed person."

President Golding pointed to her arms. The bruising was fading from her recent battle with the Black Flu, but it was still evident. "How did that happen?" he asked.

"During our journey from Chicago, we joined a group of Baptists who helped protect us. When we reached a camp near Springfield, I contracted the Black Flu and was quarantined. The people pretty much left us for dead, and I felt like I deserved it, since I'd caused Nathan all of this trouble."

President Golding raised his eyebrows. "But you're here, seemingly healthy . . ."

A tear slid down Marie's cheek. "Yes, Nathan ignored the quarantine and came to my side. He gave me a priesthood blessing, and I was healed. I suddenly felt the Lord's love like never before, and I know I still have many things to accomplish in this life. Despite my previous shortfalls, I now feel worthy to enter the temple."

"I feel you are too."

They finished the questions, and then the president briefly covered the various aspects of the ordinances she would receive that day. After about a half hour, they met Nathan outside the office.

"She passed with flying colors," President Golding said to him before adding, "I suppose I should interview you as well, unless you happen to have your recommend with you."

Nathan smiled and pulled out his wallet. He extracted a tattered but readable temple recommend and handed it to the president. "I've still got more than a year to go on this one. Don't worry, I have remained worthy."

"I'm impressed you've held onto it through everything," President Golding said. "Well, I'm sure they're ready for us now."

The next two hours were busy for Marie, who did her best to comprehend everything, and the temple workers did a fine job of guiding her through the endowment session.

∞

At the conclusion of the endowment session, everyone stepped into the Celestial Room. Nathan took Marie into his arms, and the Spirit poured forth in great abundance.

"Even with all the turmoil in the world, there can still be heaven on earth," President Golding said.

"There's still one more matter to take care of," he said, winking at Nathan. "Shall we go to one of the sealing rooms?"

Soon Nathan and Marie were kneeling across from each other at a holy altar as the others watched.

President Golding recited the words of the sealing ordinance. He concluded by saying, "You make a wonderful couple. Please come around to the front of the room so we can congratulate you once again."

As they moved across the room, Nathan put his arm around Marie and whispered, "Sorry I don't have a ring for you."

"It's okay," Marie said. "We've only been officially engaged for a few hours."

Then Marie's eyes lit up as one of the women stepped toward them with a container that held a display of various rings and said, "When the economy started falling apart, the local jeweler grabbed his best items and left town, but he forgot a cabinet full of rings in the back room. They aren't too fancy, but hopefully you'll each find one you like."

Marie sorted through the rings, and finally narrowed her choices down to two small diamond rings. "They're both beautiful," she said as she tried on the second one, "but this one fits a little better. Thank you so much."

Nathan chose a simple gold band, and they placed them on each other's fingers. Then Nathan gave Marie a big kiss as everyone smiled.

President Golding had been silent throughout the ring selection, and now to everyone's surprise he stepped forward and gave Nathan a big embrace.

He stepped back and said in a husky voice, "I apologize for that awkward hug, but that is from your mother Helen. She is with us today and wanted me to tell you she loves you both. She says you make a beautiful couple."

Nathan choked up. He hadn't told the president anything about his parents. He looked around the room. "Mom is here?"

"Yes. She says they're celebrating in your behalf in the Spirit World."

"What a wonderful wedding gift," Marie said. There wasn't a dry eye in the room as the Spirit testified of the truthfulness of the president's message from Helen.

They soon left the sealing room and stood outside the temple. It was now late afternoon, and they were all weary from the day's flurry of activity. "This has been a wonderful day that we'll never forget," President Golding said. "Thank you for letting us all be a part of it. We do have one other gift for you, though."

Another woman stepped forward and handed Nathan a key. "This is the master suite at the Hotel Nauvoo," she said. "People say Nauvoo is a nice place for a honeymoon."

The next morning Nathan and Marie were startled awake by a knock on their hotel door. Nathan jumped up and pulled his clothes on while Marie hid under the covers. Nathan opened the door to find President Golding standing there sheepishly.

"I'm so sorry to disturb you, but last evening we received some urgent messages from Church headquarters," he said. "Salt Lake was hit by a powerful earthquake yesterday, and there is a message that pertains to you. When you're dressed and ready, please come to my office."

"We'll be right there," Nathan said.

Twenty minutes later, President Golding handed Marie a printout of the message the Church had sent out about the earthquake. It told about the severe flooding and structural damage all along the Wasatch Front, as well as the growing total of those who were killed.

"This is horrible," Marie said. "I hope my parents are okay."

President Golding then handed Nathan another printout and said, "This is the one that affects you directly."

It read:

ATTENTION: ALL MAINTENANCE MISSIONARIES

This is a call for all maintenance missionaries to return to Salt Lake to assist in the recovery efforts following the recent earthquake. If you are aware of a maintenance missionary in your area, instruct him to report to Elder Wilford Miller at the Bishop's Central Storehouse in Salt Lake as soon as possible. Temple presidents and camp leaders are authorized to allow the missionary to TBV if applicable, due to the special circumstances.

Nathan and Marie looked at each other. "That's going to be a long walk," she said, "but we better go."

"What does TBV mean?" Nathan asked. "I've never seen that acronym before."

"It means 'Travel by Vehicle' if one is available," President Golding said. "You're in luck. We have several vehicles tucked away for emergencies, along with plenty of fuel."

Marie nearly collapsed with joy. "That is the best news I've ever heard."

By mid-morning, Nathan and Marie were settled into the front seat of a 2013 Ford F-150. The truck had some wear and tear on it, having been used often by the Church service missionaries during previous summers, but it felt wonderfully luxurious.

Nathan had filled some gas cans and covered them with a blanket in the back of the truck, and President Golding gave him $300 just in case the truck was a gas guzzler.

"Even with martial law going into effect, hopefully you'll be able to find some rural stores that will happily take cash," President Golding said. "Don't be too shocked at the price. The last I heard was it's more than $5 per gallon. Hopefully they won't gouge you too badly."

"There were a couple of good stations I found when I came out here," Nathan said. "I'll try to follow the same route back."

"President, thank you for everything," Marie said. "Yesterday was the highlight of my life."

"It was an honor to be a part of it," President Golding said as he reached through the truck window to shake each of their hands. "We'll be praying for you to have a safe journey."

Nathan smiled as he started the engine. "Well, there's at least one benefit to heading back to Utah," he told the president. "Now I can ask Elder Miller if it's all right to get married!"

CHAPTER 21

———————— ❧ ————————

Carol shook Denise awake just after sunrise. They were sleeping under a big pine tree about a half-mile from the remains of Deer Creek Reservoir. They had spent the night on the hill because their path was now blocked by mud in seemingly every direction.

Denise sat up with a confused look. "Where are we?"

"Don't you remember?" Carol asked. "The dam broke."

Denise simply nodded and reached into her backpack for a granola bar. "I remember now."

"I'm sorry, but there's not an easy way to the camp," Carol said as she pointed in the direction of Kamas across the valley. "We'd have to somehow hike up and around this mess."

"It will be okay," Denise said. "Let's keep walking."

They hiked along the hills south of the reservoir, and within a couple of hours they saw a paved road that seemed to magically emerge from the mud.

"I think this leads to a town called Wallsburg, tucked away behind those hills," Carol said. "Maybe someone still lives there."

As they started walking down the road, they heard a shout. They stopped in their tracks as two men holding guns approached them. They looked like a father and a son.

"Who are you?" the younger one asked.

"We're just some harmless travelers," Carol said, hoping to keep the conversation light. "We were nearly killed by the flood. Can you help us?"

"So you saw the flood?" the older man asked.

"Yes, we'd just crossed the Deer Creek Dam when the earthquake hit. The Jordanelle Dam must've burst too, because a wall of water wiped out Heber, and then slammed into Deer Creek and tore out the dam. There's no way anyone in the canyon could've survived that flood."

"That's what we figured had happened," the younger man said. "None of us saw it, though. We were too busy trying to put our camp back together after the earthquake."

"Are you part of the Wallsburg camp?" Carol asked.

"Yes. We're guarding this road," the younger man said. "Sorry, but we aren't letting anyone in right now. The camp is nearly out of food."

Carol got a little testy. "You're kidding, right? We just had a major natural disaster that destroyed the canyon. There's no reason for you to stand guard, because I promise you no one else is coming this way anytime soon."

The men didn't budge, though, until Denise put on her best puppy-dog eyes and said, "I'm so very hungry. Please take us to the camp."

The men looked at each other and shrugged. "They look fairly harmless," the older man said. "Let's take them there."

He pointed a thumb at himself and added, "I'm Jeb, and this is my son Stew."

"Nice to meet you," Carol said. "I'm Carol and this is Denise."

They started walking toward Wallsburg, and the men asked how things were going down in the valley. Carol told them about how Orem was getting more dangerous, and that the CCA was cracking down on making sure everyone had the chip.

"We just had to get out of there," Carol said. "I'm sure the flood will just add to the problems now."

Stew kept looking at them and finally blurted out, "You're not mother and daughter, are you?"

Carol laughed. "No, although it's starting to feel like it. Denise, how would you describe our relationship?"

Denise pondered for a moment. "My half-brother is very

interested in her daughter."

Jeb shrugged. "I guess that counts. Where are they at?"

"They were in Chicago the last we heard," Carol said. "We hope they got out safely, though. All the big cities are starting to flare up with riots. People are getting angry about all of the country's problems."

The camp was coming into view. There was an orderly row of tents set up, but there seemed to be a general sense of disorder to the camp. From what Carol could determine, it had to be one of the secondary camps that Nathan had talked about, rather than one where the Saints had first gathered.

Some small children approached the visitors and then tagged along behind them. Carol noticed they looked quite skinny and she wondered whether there was going to be much food to spare.

"How many people live here?" Carol asked.

"We've got about 300 people here now," Stew said. "Some families left just a couple of days ago because of the food situation. I hate to think what might have happened to them if things are as bad as you say they are."

They soon reached a large building with a sign that read, "*Wallsburg Community Center.*"

"It's almost lunchtime," Jeb said. "We eat as a group, so you can meet the other members of the camp. I think they'd like to hear what you have to say about life in the valley."

❧

Thirty minutes later, Carol and Denise had full stomachs and were now sitting in front of the residents of the Wallsburg camp, who had gathered around them. The camp didn't seem to have a true leader, but since Jeb and Stew had brought Carol and Denise to the camp, they acted as moderators.

Carol started by retelling the story of the earthquake and the flooding they had witnessed, and then gave some background on the situation in Utah County. She knew her message wasn't too hopeful, and it reflected on the faces of the residents.

"Be of good cheer," she told them. "In many ways, you're better off here than the people in the valley. I know it has been a struggle at times, but at least you're safe and don't fear that your house will be broken into by gangs. Denise and I left because the violence in my Orem neighborhood was really starting to worry us."

A woman called out, "Then what should we do? Within two weeks we'll be out of food."

"We need to put our trust in God," Denise suddenly said. "He'll help us if we rely on him."

"Denise is right," Carol said. "We need to pray for help. I don't care if you're Mormon, Catholic, or Baptist. We need to kneel down and ask our Heavenly Father to guide us in our actions, and to ask Him to send us food."

"Amen," Jeb said loudly, but the people first looked skeptical. They had been hoping for a more practical solution, but as Carol and Denise knelt down, joined by Jeb and Stew, every person was soon down on their knees.

Carol knew she needed to be the voice for the prayer, so she briefly stood and said, "I'll offer the prayer, but please be praying in your hearts as well. We need all the help we can get."

CHAPTER 22

The next morning, as Denise and Carol began their first full day helping to better organize the Wallsburg camp, Aaron was in downtown Salt Lake. He was still trying to wrap his mind around the extent of the damage that lay before him.

He had spent a sleepless night on a couch in Kathy's backyard, then after saying good-bye to Dale at sunrise, he had started walking toward Temple Square. Along the way he had talked to several people who were heading away from downtown. They told him that Temple Square and the City Creek Center were completely flooded and basically uninhabitable, but he kept going.

He eventually reached the Salt Lake Library, at the intersection of 200 East and 400 South, but the water was nearly up to his waist. The area felt abandoned, and he guessed that most people had left the area the day before.

He realized there was no point in trying to reach Temple Square. He knew that Elder Bushman, his NSA contact, lived in a home higher on the hill, directly south of the Salt Lake City Cemetery. Hopefully he could find him.

Aaron had never actually seen Elder Bushman's home, but they had corresponded so many times using their snail-mail method of sharing "baking recipes" that Aaron had his address memorized. They had met a couple of times at Church headquarters just before Aaron had received the chip, so he was confident Elder Bushman would recognize him.

An hour later, Aaron knocked on Elder Bushman's door. He noticed a tree leaning against the garage and a two-foot-wide crack in the driveway, but otherwise the home looked okay.

He saw a man peering out of the window, and Aaron called out, "It's me, Aaron Shaw!"

The door soon opened, and Elder Bushman moved forward to shake Aaron's hand.

"I wasn't sure I'd ever hear from you again," Elder Bushman said. "It sounds like the south end of the valley got hammered."

"Everything got hammered," Aaron replied. "We've got our hands full for months to come."

"Come inside," Elder Bushman said. "Nothing works, but at least we can sit down out of the sun. You're probably starving."

He went to the kitchen and brought Aaron some cookies and a bottle of water, then he shared what he knew.

"Many Church leaders are unaccounted for right now," he said. "Temple Square and the other buildings downtown were hit hard by the flooding. I haven't been down there, but they say the water is up to the first set of windows on the temple. If that's true, there are going to be a lot of casualties."

"I believe it," Aaron said. "I made it all the way to the Salt Lake Library, but the water just kept getting deeper."

Aaron then took a few minutes to share what he had experienced the past two days, beginning with the troubles at the NSA Data Center and the huge sinkhole at the south end of the valley.

"So you actually saw the sinkhole?" Elder Bushman asked.

"I stood right on the edge, and I couldn't see any signs of life," Aaron said. "The damage is unbelievable."

"Wow. I'm not sure where we'll even begin in terms of rebuilding things," Elder Bushman said. "We've got a long road ahead of us."

"What are the Church's plans in terms of rebuilding? Can we use the people up in the camps to help us out?"

Elder Bushman shrugged. "That's definitely a possibility, although some of those camps already have other assignments ahead of them. You might remember that we labeled the mountain camps as either white camps or blue camps."

"Yes," Aaron said. "The white camps are where the Saints live who first heeded the prophet's call to gather."

"That's right, and from all reports, those Saints are doing well," Elder Bushman said. "In fact, it's almost time for those camps to join together into larger groups in the next few weeks before winter arrives. For example, most of the white camps south of Point of the Mountain will travel to Sanpete County soon and settle near the Manti Temple. Then next spring they'll hopefully be able to start the trek to Missouri."

Aaron smiled. "I sometimes forget we've got bigger building projects ahead of us."

"Yes, New Jerusalem must be built, no matter what other obstacles are thrown at us along the way."

"Then what about the blue camps?" Aaron asked.

"As you know, those camps weren't as heavily stocked with supplies, and they aren't governed by priesthood leadership. We've had reports that some camps are starting to run out of food, and there's been some violent clashes within the camps as well."

"That's crazy," Aaron said. "Is it really so hard for people to just get along?"

"Apparently so, but those camps will be formally disbanded as soon as possible. People can continue living at the camps if they want, but they'll be encouraged to return to the valleys and help with the rebuilding process. We think most of them will take that option."

"I agree," Aaron said. "It sounds like they're suffering from cabin fever."

"A majority of the people in those camps are LDS," Elder Bushman said. "So when they return, we'll reestablish functioning wards with newly called leaders."

"That's good to hear," Aaron said. "As you know, I've visited some of the current wards, and we're on the verge of apostasy in most cases."

"We knew that would happen, but we had to let those wards coast along with the hope that new leadership would return from the blue camps. They aren't the strongest members, obviously, or else they would've gone to the white camps, but the Lord is merciful and He will help his Saints as much as they will allow him to."

"I'm glad to hear that," Aaron said. "I'm concerned about the U.N.'s plans, though. You probably didn't receive my last letter. It would've arrived yesterday."

Elder Bushman shook his head. "I didn't. What did it say?"

"Well, I wrote that we're going to receive some additional help here in the valley, whether we want it or not. During my final days at the data center, we received word that a large group of U.N. forces in Los Angeles were planning to move further inland along I-15 toward Las Vegas, even before the earthquake struck here. Since their leaders love to take over disaster zones, they've probably already added Salt Lake as a must-see destination."

Elder Bushman frowned. "That's bad news. We were hoping they'd forget about us out here in the desert."

"Don't count on it."

"Then we'll need your expertise to prepare for their arrival," Elder Bushman said. "You and I need to reach Church headquarters in the next couple of days—even if it is by canoe."

CHAPTER 23

Nathan and Marie left Nauvoo and found a bridge across the Mississippi River into Iowa. They had brought some maps with them, and Nathan was soon following the same roads he'd taken on his journey to Chicago.

"It's a great relief to be heading back to Utah with you at my side," Nathan told her. "I was terrified I'd never find you. I'll thank the Lord for the rest of my life for bringing us together again."

Once in a while they had to pass through some small towns, and Marie was bothered by the scenes on the streets. In many cases, it was like coming upon a murder scene before the police had arrived, except in these cases the police were never going to come. The bodies they encountered were going to continue decomposing along the road for the foreseeable future.

"I didn't realize Nauvoo was such an oasis of peace," Marie said as she recoiled from yet another grisly sight. "There really must be angels watching over that town."

"I'm certain of that," Nathan replied.

When they were loading the truck, Nathan had noticed a Book of Mormon under the seat. He now asked Marie to grab it.

"Turn to Ether 2:9-10," he said. "I've pondered these verses a lot since being called as a maintenance missionary. I think we're seeing them being fulfilled."

Marie turned to the page and read aloud:

"And now, we can behold the decrees of God concerning this land, that it is a land of promise; and whatsoever nation shall possess it shall serve God, or they shall be swept off when the fulness of his wrath shall

come upon them. And the fulness of his wrath cometh upon them when they are ripened in iniquity.

"For behold, this is a land which is choice above all other lands; wherefore he that doth possess it shall serve God or shall be swept off; for it is the everlasting decree of God. And it is not until the fulness of iniquity among the children of the land, that they are swept off."

Nathan turned to look at her. "Don't you agree that we're witnessing that cleansing now?" he asked. "But it is comforting to know that things will be better afterward."

"I truly hope so," Marie said.

As they traveled, Nathan was grateful the government still hadn't installed checkpoints at the state lines on the rural roads. Their stops for gas at out-of-the-way stations were rather uneventful, and the store employees always eagerly accepted the cash. Nathan figured it was because they didn't need to report it to the government. They could just pocket the money for themselves.

They did have some trouble during one fill-up, but Marie always turned on the chip detector whenever they were stopped. The scanner alerted her that two men were running toward them from a nearby building just as Nathan finished filling the tank.

"Get in the truck!" she shouted, and they peeled away just as the men reached them. One took a swing with a baseball bat and dented the truck's tailgate, but Nathan quickly left them in the dust.

They soon reached southern Wyoming and crossed into Utah. They passed through the towns of Vernal and Roosevelt, and then drove near Strawberry Reservoir. There seemed to be a lot more tents than usual along the shore.

As they headed toward the canyon that led to Heber, though, there was a barricade across the road. There was a family standing along the road, and Nathan rolled down his window.

"Why can't we go this way?" he asked an older man.

The man looked at him in surprise. "Haven't you heard? Heber was destroyed by a flood. The Jordanelle Dam broke."

Nathan shook his head. "Wow. I didn't know that. We've been

out of the area. So we're stuck here?"

He shook his head. "You can go back the way you came, or take one of the dirt roads off the beaten path, but there's no guarantee you'll make it through. We've had some people say they had to turn around because of some pretty big cracks in the road from the earthquake."

"Where do the roads lead to?" Marie asked. "My parents are in Orem. We're just trying to get there."

The man turned and pointed west. "Somewhere over there is a road that will take you to Wallsburg. If anyone is still living there, they could give you directions from that point."

Nathan smiled when he heard the word "Wallsburg."

"Thank you for your help," he told the man. "We'll at least give it a try."

He steered the truck in the general area the man had pointed and saw a dirt road leading off into the hills.

"Are you sure this is a good idea?" Marie asked. "What if no one is there?"

"We're going to be all right," Nathan responded. "I led a group of people to a camp in Wallsburg not too long ago. Most of them were members of the Church. We'll find friends there to help us."

Unfortunately, they soon learned the road through the mountains above Wallsburg was as bad as the man had described. Sometimes Nathan had to push boulders out of the way to even get the truck past them, and there were some drop-offs that made Marie silently scream as they inched past them. Thankfully they still had some full gas cans in the back of the truck, because they were burning through fuel quickly due to their slow pace.

Nathan kept driving for an hour after sunset, but he finally realized they had to stop for the night to avoid driving off the road.

"Did we make the right choice?" Marie asked more than once, but Nathan assured her they were going to be okay.

❦

The next morning they reached a stretch of road where they could coast downhill, and Nathan occasionally caught glimpses of the back of Mount Timpanogos in the distance.

"We're getting close," he said as they came out of a grove of trees. "Look! There's Wallsburg just ahead!"

Marie looked at the cluster of buildings and tents and couldn't hold back the tears.

"Thank thee, Heavenly Father," she prayed. "Please let these people be kind to us."

The truck stirred up plenty of dust as it approached the town, and dozens of people came outside to see what was causing all of the commotion. Nathan noticed a few of the men were carrying shotguns, and he wisely stopped the truck a hundred yards from the closest tents.

"Let's get out slowly with our hands up," he told Marie. "There's no need to get shot."

They got out of the truck and walked slowly toward the group. "We come in peace," Nathan called out. "We are only seeking to find a way to Utah Valley."

As they got closer, one of the women said, "Hey, aren't you Elder Foster, the missionary who led us here in the first place?"

Nathan looked closely at the woman and recognized her as the lady he had talked to at the Provo Temple gate before leading her group to Wallsburg.

"I am," Nathan said. "I'm so happy to see you're still doing fine."

"You probably know that Provo Canyon is a mess right now," one of the men said. "We just had a woman and a girl come that way a few days ago who said it was a giant mud pit. You're welcome to talk to them about whether they think you could get a truck down there."

"I'd like to do that," Nathan said. "Where are they?"

The man led them to a small tent and said, "I think they're napping right now, but go ahead and check."

Marie stepped forward. "Let me do it. They might respond

better to a feminine voice."

She pulled the tent flap aside, and then let out a scream. The two people in the tent had seen her and screamed as well. Then Marie dived into the tent, and Nathan stood outside in shock.

"Marie, what's going on?" he asked nervously. Suddenly Marie reached through the flap and pulled him in by the front of his shirt. He found himself face to face with Marie's mom Carol.

"I don't believe it," he cried as she gave him a hug.

He looked past her and saw his sister Denise sitting there with tears streaming down her cheeks. "Nathan! I've missed you so much!"

The man outside finally stuck his head into the tent. He looked absolutely bewildered. "Is everything all right?"

"Jeb, everything is marvelous," Carol said. "This is my daughter Marie and her boyfriend Nathan. This is unbelievable!"

The man motioned for them to come out of the tent. "This calls for a celebration!"

They all happily climbed out of the tent and began following Jeb toward the main building. Carol instinctively clutched Marie's hand and felt a ring.

"What's this?" she asked in surprise. "Are you two engaged?"

Nathan smiled mischievously. "Even better. We're married."

Carol stopped in her tracks with her mouth open, unsure to be happy or outraged.

"Mom, we got sealed in the Nauvoo Temple," Marie said. "Everything is wonderful."

Carol couldn't contain herself and threw her arms around them both, and Denise joined in the group hug.

"I don't know if I can take any more surprises," Carol finally said. "Let's go eat."

CHAPTER 24

Garrett Foster was still in spiritual turmoil as he helped lead a squadron of U.N. peacekeepers up I-15 toward Nevada. They had navigated the cracked freeway through Los Angeles' eastern suburbs, then climbed up the canyon onto the plateau near Victorville. The whole area was blackened after a raging wildfire had recently swept through the area.

He finally rationalized that he hadn't denied the existence of God or done anything that might jeopardize his eternal welfare. He had simply committed to devote all his time, talents and resources to the Coalition.

"It's a man-made organization and will someday fall," he told himself. "I'm only doing this to reach my children."

They stopped briefly in Barstow at sunset, but if anyone was living there, they weren't showing their faces to the U.N. personnel. Then they got back onto I-15, and the U.N.'s amazing five-axel trucks just kept plowing forward at 35 miles per hour through the night.

By the next morning they had crested the last hill before reaching the Nevada state line, and they rolled into Primm an hour later. The town had never been much more than a tourist trap and gambling stop in the first place, and it had clearly been several weeks since anyone had been there. The wind had already blown several inches of desert sand across the parking lots.

He stepped out of his transport vehicle and walked with Commander Klopov toward Whisky Pete's Casino, which already looked like an ancient ruin.

"We had heard the Black Flu really affected Nevada," Klopov told him. "People from Los Angeles fled this direction and carried the disease with them. The mortality rate was sky high."

They stepped into the casino, but the stench of death was strong, and they could see bodies scattered throughout the building's interior.

"It looks like your report about the Black Flu was correct," Garrett said.

When they returned to the vehicles, an officer rushed up to Klopov. "You have an urgent call from Coalition headquarters."

Klopov excused himself, and took the call. He returned twenty minutes later. He looked delighted, but he didn't give Garrett any hint of what he was talking about.

"You look very happy, sir," Garrett told him. "Can't you share the news with me?"

"Sorry, but you'll find out tomorrow, along with the rest of America," Klopov said.

They reached Las Vegas that evening. The famous Vegas Strip and all the glitzy hotels were dark, but there were a few neighborhoods in the city of Henderson where the lights were on. They proceeded in that direction and talked to several residents who said they'd been able to keep their power on because Hoover Dam was still partially operational.

Garrett was relieved to see at least one U.S. city that was actually functioning. He had started to worry that America was now just a wasteland, but it was clear that some communities were still working together.

The U.N. peacekeepers decided to spend the night at the Hilton Garden Inn, and the hotel owners did all they could to please their new guests. Garrett was given his own room, and all he wanted to do was watch TV. The power had never been fully restored in Los Angeles, so he had been out of the loop for months in terms of national news. He'd been living in a U.N.-based fantasy world.

Of course, the news coverage he was able to find on TV felt unreal to him as well. The chirpy TV news anchors talked happily about how the U.N. peacekeepers had saved the day. They said the government was predicting modest economic growth through the end of the year, and one smiling anchorman even said, "By Christmas we should be back to the America we all remember."

Garrett couldn't help but scoff at that statement, but as he flipped through the channels, the same cheerful message was being shared.

In the back of his mind, though, was Klopov's beaming face earlier that day. Something wasn't right. Whatever secret he was holding probably didn't include a happy Christmas for America.

~

The next morning as Garrett left his room and entered the hotel lobby, he saw several people crowded around the TV. He stepped closer and saw the words "Oil Freeze" across the bottom of the screen.

"What's going on?" Garrett asked a man who had been watching the TV intently.

The man shook his head without turning to realize he was talking to a U.N. officer. "Those jerks in the Middle East are cutting off our oil supply. Can you believe it?"

"I can," Garrett said with a frown.

The man turned to look at him and nearly swallowed his tongue. "Oh, I'm so sorry," the man said, practically bowing down to him. "I didn't mean it."

"Don't sweat it," Garrett said. He walked out of the lobby and found Klopov sitting inside their transport vehicle. The Russian looked at him with delight and said, "Did you hear the news?"

"Yes," Garrett said as a wave of mixed emotions passed through him. "I suppose this was the big surprise you were talking about yesterday."

Klopov laughed. "Americans are so foolish. They actually think we wanted to help them. We're not here to save America—we're here to take control of America. This is the first step."

Garrett involuntary winced, and Klopov noticed. He stared into Garrett's eyes as he put his hand on his pistol. "I like you, Foster, but can I trust you? This is your time of decision. Are you an American or are you part of the Coalition?"

Garrett breathed out slowly. "I am devoted to the Coalition."

"That's what I wanted to hear," Klopov said. He stood up and put his hand on Garrett's shoulder. "All of our intelligence reports say there is one place that will oppose us more than anywhere else. Any guesses where that is?"

"Utah."

"Correct," Klopov said with a grin. "Your home. The earthquake there has left them vulnerable, and you're going to lead us right into the heart of Salt Lake—so we can rip it out."

A Nation in Upheaval

The oil embargo's effect on America was immediate. Within hours, the price of gasoline began to climb drastically, Seemingly everyone who owned a car rushed to the nearest gas station to get any remaining fuel. Some lines stretched for 10 blocks, even though it was clear that the gas supply would run out long before the cars at the end of the line could be filled.

The U.S. president assured the nation that everything possible was being done to resume the oil shipments, but his promises were hollow. The Coalition's plan to cripple the United States had worked even better than they had expected, and the great American giant was suddenly very vulnerable.

The first outward signs of a national collapse came with the reports of riots and even gang warfare sprouting up throughout the nation. In Washington, D.C., mobs rallied in front of the Capitol Building and the White House, blaming the federal government for the situation.

Violent protests were organized throughout the nation, where citizens demanded that the country begin drilling for oil immediately, but it was an unrealistic hope. Nearly all of the oil wells in the U.S. had been damaged by either Hurricane Barton or The Great Storm.

As the country's difficulties escalated, Washington D.C. became the target of disgruntled citizens. Violence spread throughout the city, and the nation's leaders went into hiding, fearing the worst. The president's cabinet members and key Congressional leaders convened at a secret, top-security bunker in Virginia, where they would live for the foreseeable future. Under this arrangement, the federal government continued to exist on a minimal level, but out of sight from the citizens.

They were in contact with the top military generals, but America faced a serious problem—most of the nation's armed forces were overseas fighting other people's battles. Very few troops were available on U.S. soil to help quell the violence—or heaven forbid, to defend the country against an attack from a foreign power. America was at a boiling point, and the pot was about to boil over.

The Coalition leaders watched these developments and knew it was time to provide their U.N. peacekeepers with additional help.

World War III was on the horizon.

Don't miss what lies ahead for the Foster and Shaw families as the *Times of Turmoil* series continues in *Book Three: Days of Fury.*

BONUS SECTION

As I mentioned in the Author's Note at the front of this book, I would encourage you to read *The Spirit of Liberty* by Suzanne Freeman.

At the conclusion of *The Renewed Earth*, the final volume in the *Standing in Holy Places* series, I included the first chapter of Suzanne's book *Through the Window of Life,* because her inspiring and important message about the future had helped me create that series.

In a similar way, *The Spirit of Liberty* seems to apply directly to this new series. I have received permission from the author and the publisher to include a chapter from the book that explains how the U.S. government will soon use tyranny and martial law to exercise power over the people.

If you are looking for additional insight into the lives of the Founding Fathers—as well as the future of the United States—don't hesitate to read Suzanne's latest book.

Thanks again for your support of my novels!

Chad Daybell

THE SPIRIT OF LIBERTY

My Vision of America's Future

by Suzanne Freeman

Toward the end of my visit with America's founders, I asked Jesus, "What is America's future?" I wasn't certain I really wanted to know. You'd think I would've learned not to ask questions, because sometimes I get answers that are difficult to accept.

I had learned that Jesus didn't force difficult information on me. The desire for such knowledge had to come from within my heart, and after I asked the question, he would provide the answer.

The Savior explained to me that there are multiple choices and possible outcomes in America's future. There could even be a combination of these results, but there were three scenarios that were shown to me.

I was taught that we never truly know the exact future because our individual and collective choices change the outcome. If we make certain choices, one thing could happen and if we made another choice, a different event could occur. I was told that nothing is set in stone, other than the Savior will come again at the Second Coming in all of His glory.

So we can change what will happen with our choices, and that means we are more powerful than we think we are. We have the power to shape the course of the future.

When Jesus showed me the vision, He looked upon me with great love and kindness. It made me wish that everyone on earth

155

could understand the greatness of His love. I knew He didn't want his children to suffer more than what was needed for our growth and understanding. Without that growth and understanding, we would not progress in our spiritual development or cry to Him in prayer. I could feel his love and hope for those who would hear the messages of warning that the Heavens were sending to the earth.

I know Christ showed me this vision so we could understand that we have the power to choose, even though "the powers that be" seem to make the choices for us. I also saw that He will prepare places of safety for the righteous to escape the challenging times that will soon be upon us. These are places where we will have love and joy while awaiting the Coming of the Lord.

I was shown a few different ways in which the future might develop according to the decisions we will make. Even these results could vary, and I did not see everything. I only know what my understanding of the future was at the time of this vision.

There are things I don't understand and therefore I might not have noted every possible angle. I also see things through the optimism of rose-colored glasses, and I have a hard time focusing on the bad and ugly, so I tend not to report those aspects. I can look at these difficult things when I have to, because I know that through faith, anything is possible. We grow through adversity and I have certainly grown from the things the Lord has taught me, even the difficult and frightening things.

When I was shown the different ways America could fall, I learned that some people would not have to endure the coming difficulties exactly the same way as the unprepared will. Although they might not have the type of home or food they were used to, they did have a sense of peace that could only come from above. They had a perfect knowledge that there would be something great coming, and that it would be necessary for our learning and development.

If there is hope, there is peace. I know this, and I saw it happen over and over in the vision that Jesus gave me. I saw angels of peace coming to help those who had faith and hope even in the most difficult. When there was hope, there was help.

I could see that those with hope had the spirit of liberty shining in their hearts. It was a gift from the Heavens that could never be taken from them.

I knew that America had reached this point of vulnerability through a series of decisions, particularly after the beginning of the 21st Century. The United States had weathered other challenging times, such as the Great Depression in the 1930s, the Watergate crisis in the 1970s, and the Iran-Contra scandal in the 1980s.

However, it was the attacks that occurred on September 11, 2001 that launched America on its current course. That tragedy sparked the creation of the Patriot Act, which has led to greater government involvement and scrutiny of the everyday lives of Americans. The attacks also sparked the reorganization of many U.S. government agencies, and in 2003 the United States Department of Homeland Security was formed with the goal of reducing terrorism within the United States. These decisions by our national leaders were well-intentioned, but they have led to situations that could potentially limit or even take away our liberty.

Both the George W. Bush and Barack Obama presidential administrations greatly expanded the government's reach through executive orders and other mandates that have led us to our current situation. President Obama's election in 2012 to a second term in office means the same tactics will likely continue.

As I was shown the events of our country's future, I understood that it is important to know how to listen to the Spirit of the Lord, and to make sure that we do as He directs. This will help us to know what to do when difficult situations arise. There is always a way out of difficulties for those who know how to follow the Spirit of God.

As you read this, please keep in mind that these things do not have to happen in the exact way that I saw them in vision. These are only *possibilities* based upon our changeable decisions. So with that being said, I will tell you what I learned while I was in the presence of the Lord.

TYRANNY

It has been said, "A caged canary is secure; but it is not free. It is easier for free men to resist terrorism from afar than tyranny from within." [1]

The first scenario I was shown was one of total tyranny in which our rights as U.S. citizens were completely taken away by our own government. I was shown that it happened gradually in a way that initially sounded good, as if they were doing us a favor, while their actions were really designed to remove our freedoms. People didn't realize it until it was too late.

It occurred to me that it was like plucking a wing feather, once a day, from a beautiful bird. The bird can still fly until too many wing feathers are plucked, then suddenly the bird has lost the power of flight.

The government will further mislead the citizens by saying that we would all be better off if we helped each other by merely pooling our resources together.

As I watched this possible outcome unfold, I saw a few good people who helped one another, but more often I saw people not wanting to help a stranger. These people were selfish, and this selfishness made it easy for the government leaders to take over and give power to the rich and the thoughtless.

Those seeking power became wealthy, and they took control over the rights of the common people. This was a great surprise to those who wanted to get government help. They were promised many things, but the flamboyant person serving as president took control and did what he wanted to serve himself, all the while stealing from the common man. All he cared for was becoming a man of power.

Children were taught in school to get a job, and to never start their own businesses. The government purposefully made it difficult to own a small business. There was greed, control, and corruption, and while big industries prospered, the people were pushed deeper into poverty. It was explained to me that the government is a reflection of the people. If the people are wicked and corrupt, their government will be also.

I saw brightness around some people. They still had hope, even during the difficult times. They trusted in God and made the choice to be happy, while they waited for God to deliver them.

I hope that this wonderful country can be saved. I look at the inspirational examples of our Founding Fathers, and people like Joan of Arc. They changed the course of history through the spirit of liberty burning strong in their hearts. I am convinced that if we take the spirit of liberty into our hearts, we will have freedom in any situation. Margaret Mead once said, "A small group of thoughtful people could change the world. Indeed, it's the only thing that ever has."[2]

Then the vision shifted and I saw another future possibility being portrayed.

PROMISED HELP NOT FORTHCOMING

In this scenario, I was shown that people wanted to have as much help as possible from the government with food, housing, and health care. So they elected a president they thought would do just that—help the people. But when he became president he didn't do what he had promised, and he didn't care about the common person. All he wanted was power, and the decisions he made caused the people to suffer greatly.

Food got even more expensive, and wages did not follow inflation. The food costs were so high that it wasn't long before the children went hungry. Many citizens would go to bed starving each night. It was a great surprise to the people how quickly this happened.

Health care was practically unavailable. If a child broke his arm there was no way to get the help he needed. People had to sign up on a long waiting list for medical treatment, and it didn't matter how urgent the injury was, they still had to wait their turn. A broken arm was not considered an emergency.

Prescription medications were hard to get, and strong pain medications were illegal. The government controlled these things, and the people who needed them the most could not get them. The black market was big, and for a high price, they sold things that are easily bought in stores today.

Most women today have their babies in the hospital, but not in this scenario. Birthing was not considered a medical emergency, and doctors were not allowed to conduct births in the hospitals.

I saw some doctors sneak around and deliver babies at home, but there was a big fine and jail time for them if they were caught. Some compassionate doctors felt it was worth the risk, feeling there had to be someone to help babies arrive safely into this world.

Doctors weren't the only ones helping. I saw people taking care of each other. I was shown people who sacrificed material possessions and did good deeds for others. As midwives have done for thousands of years, there were trained people who knew how to assist with home births. It had to be secret, but they accepted this risk. Bartering was the only way to pay for their efforts.

There is hope and peace in knowing that even if we can't have our usual situations, there are alternatives to be found. When I saw something bad in the vision, there was always an answer somewhere, and someone who helped, even if it was not in the traditional way. There are those who were skilled, and who shared their skills with others. They knew what to do to help someone with a broken arm, a home birth, or whatever was needed. There is always an answer if we have faith.

I saw many miracles happen that illustrated this truth. In one miracle, I saw myself feeding family members as well as strangers. I opened a gallon-sized can of corn, and poured it into a four-gallon stockpot to make corn chowder.

My house was full of people walking, talking, and sitting. I looked through my kitchen and out of my dining room window to see tents, and even more people in my yard. These people were refugees from some event that wasn't made known to me. I just knew they were hungry.

I prayed while I made the soup. I told the Lord that I'd feed every hungry person who came to me if He would be kind enough to stretch the food. I just knew there would be enough.

I stood and ladled out soup. I sliced my homemade bread, and I gave each person a slice with their corn chowder. They all ate in shifts, and someone washed the bowls as fast as they were used. Some families even brought their own dishes.

The people were courteous, and they waited until everyone had eaten before they came back for more. If they wanted seconds, they got seconds, and everyone got their fill.

I told people to spread the word that we had food to share. I poured soup into other pots, and sent them outside to feed those beyond my doors.

The soup never got low until I noticed there were only a few people left in line. It ran out just as the last person left the line. Three loaves of bread and four gallons of soup had fed hundreds of people. This was one of the many miracles I was shown that taught me to trust in God for help. He will help His people.

The vision continued, showing me that righteous people lived their lives as if the government was not there. This did not make the government happy, and they could see that these people were prospering, even though they had no money. So the government made laws that there couldn't be any trading, bartering, or exchanging of services or goods of any kind. There were also rewards given to those who caught people engaging in such activities.

I saw it was common for the government to want to control everything in the people's lives. The government made it very difficult to get anything. This was not the "land of the free" anymore. This was a land of sadness.

There was no middle class. The rich got richer, while the poor were undernourished and couldn't get the necessities of life. There were so many rules and regulations for food stamps that they were very hard to get. It seemed the people who needed them the most could never get them. Even things that were needed for bare survival were not allowed at times.

This was the way the evil leaders controlled the average citizens—by fear and deprivation. There were many government workers, and the government had control of everything, even the amount of food that was allowed per person. This rationing was also used to punish large families, and they would only be allowed enough food for a smaller family. There was a limit of people per household. So if there was a family of eight, but the limit was six, the family of eight would only be allowed enough food to feed six.

Divine intervention made the food stretch, and those with hope and faith had enough to feed their large families, and their children were not hungry. God always takes care of His children.

When I looked at the people I saw two groups. Some were walking around as usual, but I could see their spirits were asleep. They were not listening to God. It was kind of funny to see these people. It was as if they had two heads, a normal one that was upright, and a spirit one that was bent over with eyes closed.

Then there were those whose spirits were wide awake and knew what was going on. They waited for knowledge, inspiration, and direction from God. They sought to learn what to do, and how to help those who were spiritually asleep.

I also could see the beautiful brightness of these people. They were far brighter than the people who were asleep. I could see that they had the Light of Christ within them. It was distinct, and they shone like Jesus did. It was like they were in eternal happiness. Jesus loved them, and they loved Jesus.

They knew that God would open a way for them and help them, so they had no despair, and this was a great gift that the government couldn't take away from them.

It didn't matter which church they attended, it only mattered that they knew God, loved Him, and would follow Him even unto death. This was a rare thing to see, and gave them a brightness of spirit that was visible. When Jesus pointed out these people to me, He explained that it was the love inside of them, which shined so brightly that I could see it.

The government would imprison those who spoke up against them. If people knew of anyone who disagreed, there would be a reward for turning them in. This made it very difficult to have personal freedoms.

But even with all the adversity, these God-loving people knew that there was a way out, and that God would take care of them. They knew it didn't matter what happened to them, only that they were right with God, and did as He commanded. They had happiness in their homes, but for most people there was never a smile out in public. It was as though it was illegal to be happy. Most people's faces reflected fear, worry and depression.

I was also shown that the people who knew God had liberty with them, and were in safe havens. They were happy, and joyous. These people had dreams and visions, guiding them on what to do. As they prayed, I could see the light that came from their prayers, and it ascended to Heaven. This was wonderful, because when a prayer was said, I saw an angel sent specifically to carry out that request.

The faith in this group was great, and they knew that there was nothing essential that God would not provide. The faith in this group was so powerful that nothing could stop them. No high-tech detecting device the government could create was as powerful as the simple faith in that group. There were many in this faithful group, but to my sadness they were few in comparison to the millions who would not hear the promptings of Jesus.

The government knew that the God-fearing people existed, but the amazing thing was that no amount of technology could ever find them. Not even airplanes or heat-searching cameras could find them, for there was a cloak of protection over the Children of God. He made them safe. His power is greater than any oppressor.

I learned that even when evil is seemingly in control, that God is really in charge, and will help those who trust in Him through miracles, and divine guidance. His plans truly are greater than our dreams.

The vision shifted again and another possible scenario opened up.

MARTIAL LAW

I saw the United States' government had decided they were the police of the world. They would go into countries and do what they wanted without regard to that country's wishes. This made these countries angry, and in retaliation, America was invaded. Our armed forces were so busy in other lands that there was not enough protection on our own soil. The citizens' guns had been taken away, so there was no way families could defend themselves against the invaders.

I was saddened to see American citizens taken away to concentration camps. There was so much bloodshed that it ran down the streets. The invaders took great joy in killing children in front of their mothers' tearful eyes. Hunger and fear were everywhere.

There were those who were given direction from God to leave the cities and go to safe places that He led them to. I could see groups fleeing and following as the Spirit directed. I could see angels guarding them. They protected them with a whisper in an ear, or sometimes they would just point in the direction that the Heavens wanted them to go, and their leaders would go that way.

This was so comforting to me to see the Lord providing an escape from danger. There was a peace that I cannot describe, a peace that can only be found from Heaven.

When I was watching the Founding Fathers' lives, I could see the angels who were helping them make the choices that were needed to create the country we have today. This is what is happening in our day. There are people who can follow the Spirit's promptings and recognize the calling that God has given them. They know what needs to be done, and they will follow the Spirit and do it. I was shown that we can have God's help if we will ask Him for it. If we as a nation just seek God in a humble way we can have His direction, protection, and help.

I saw that people that followed God's promptings shared what they had, and there was not a lot of poor, because of this unselfishness among God's children.

I did not see a nation like it is now. Evil had taken over the country so deeply and completely in many ways, including the media. Most of the people were so wicked that the majority didn't want—or didn't know how—to have a God-centered life.

I saw that this country will never be the same, because of the evil doings of rich men, but we can have peace if we are a God-loving people. There is always hope in Christ. If we have hope God will provide for us as He did for the Children of Israel. In the end it doesn't matter what the government is doing, it only matters what we do, and if we are right with God.

Christopher Columbus had a vision of this great land, and the Holy Spirit prompted his journey that led to Europe's discovery of the New World. He once wrote: "I am a most noteworthy sinner, but I have cried out to the Lord for grace and mercy, and they have covered me completely. I have found the sweetest consolation since I made it my whole purpose to enjoy His marvelous Presence."[3]

The Pilgrims and others who were brought to this Land of Promise also knew it. Likewise, we also can know what our purpose is in regard to our nation.

God has a plan for us and for this country. I saw hope in this land, even after it was filled with wickedness. It will prosper and be great again. Our country was founded on liberty, and it will stay a land of liberty. If we stay with the right, and know that God is on our side, we will see good prevail, and evil will destroy evil. As it says in Psalms 145:20, "The Lord preserveth all them that love him; but all the wicked will he destroy."

There is a spirit of liberty—a freedom to live our lives as we choose—in all of us who love God. We all have that light. We just have to search for it within ourselves. It is part of our humanness, and what sets us apart from the beast. We humans feel, choose, and love, like no other creation on earth does. We are designed by God, and He gave us the right to feel liberty deep within our souls.

We all have to find our purpose, and why we are here. It is not always to be lived just for ourselves or our families, but also to help mankind. It only takes a few people to inspire others to find liberty, both for now, and in the future.

I ask all who read this book, to find that spirit of liberty within you, and help protect the freedoms that were given to us at such a great cost. We can't give up what Thomas Jefferson, George Washington, and others worked so hard to give to us. Let us remember what they have done for us.

Some people live without regard to their freedoms, and forget the future. Those who remember history know if freedom is not cherished, and if we don't respect the things that our forefathers did, our liberties could be lost.

We must all find that spirit of liberty within us, then and only then can we ever be free. You understand that we are only free, if in our hearts we are free. So in the end it truly is our choice; it is the lives we live that will determine if we have a free country with God in charge, or if we will allow ourselves to be in bondage. I say if we are free or not, it is up to us.

We can, one person at a time, change the outcome for millions. Pray and ask God to help you find the mission that has been placed within you. You will have to reach deep within yourself and find that strength you have, and I know it's there.

There are those who will not care to search for the spirit of liberty—and there were some with this attitude in 1776—but I encourage you to not give up just because some people don't understand. Who knows? It might be *you* that can change the hearts of other people. Understand that God has a plan for you. He has faith in humanity, and He has never lost hope in us.

Samuel Adams said, "I conceive that we cannot better express ourselves than by humbly supplicating the Supreme Ruler of the world that the rod of tyrants may be broken to pieces, and the oppressed made free again; that wars may cease in all the earth, and that the confusions that are and have been among nations may be overruled by promoting and speedily bringing on that holy and happy period when the kingdom of our Lord and Saviour Jesus Christ may be everywhere established, and all people everywhere willingly bow to the sceptre of Him who is Prince of Peace."[4]

So we have our lessons to learn, and my prayer is we learn them quickly before it is too late. We must follow the Savior, be unselfish, listen to the promptings God sends us, and stand up to protect our liberties.

I know that God is on our side. We can keep this land God's country so that the flag of freedom can fly until the Savior comes.

Notes

1. Chuck Baldwin www.cancertutor.com/Quotes/Quotes_Patriotic.html
2. www.brainyquote.com/quotes/quotes/m/margaretme100502.html
3. www.brainyquote.com/quotes/authors/c/christopher_columbus.html
4. www.ringthebellsoffreedom.com/Quotes/sadamscontent.htm

ABOUT THE AUTHOR

Chad Daybell has worked in the publishing business for the past two decades and has written more than 25 books.

The *Times of Turmoil* series is a sequel to Chad's bestselling *Standing in Holy Places* series, which continues to find success in both the LDS bookstores and the national retail chains.

Chad is also known for his other novels such as *Chasing Paradise* and *The Emma Trilogy*, as well as his non-fiction books for youth, including *The Aaronic Priesthood* and *The Youth of Zion*. He and his wife Tammy also created the *Tiny Talks* series for Primary children.

Chad has worked in the publishing business for the past three decades. He is currently the president of Spring Creek Book Company. Visit **www.springcreekbooks.com** to see the company's lineup of titles.

Learn about Chad and the upcoming volumes in the *Times of Turmoil* series at his personal website **www.cdaybell.com**.